3 COLORS TRILOGY
BOOK 1

A LITTLE RED

BY

BETHANY MAINES

Blue Zephyr Press
2661 N. Pearl, #360
Tacoma WA 98407

Cover art by **LILTdesign.com**.

DEDICATED

With many thanks to Laurie Ryan who made time for all of my crazy characters.

contents

A LITTLE RED

EPISODE 1

ALLURE

Liam

Liam Grayson pulled his head out of the annual report, ears lifting at the sound of someone crying. He got up from his desk and looked around for his suit jacket and then dismissed the need for it. He was used to trying to maintain the illusion of civility, but after-work hours on Friday—on Halloween no less—didn't really call for a full suit.

He opened his office door and looked across the area that was subdivided by cubicles. The only person present on the floor was ten feet away from him at her desk. Scarlet Lucas, his secretary and midnight fantasy for the last month, was wearing a red and white checked gingham dress with a plethora of fluffy petticoats. Over the top, she had draped an itty-bitty red cloak and hood that didn't go down any further than the hem of her skirts, which ended barely below the ass he'd been drooling over since she'd been assigned to him. She had paired the entire costume with knee-high socks and red Converse. She was also sniffling into a tissue as she rifled through her desk drawer.

"Scarlet?"

She whirled around, her golden braids flying out.

"Mr. Grayson?"

"Are you all right?"

He took a step forward and caught the bright scent of fresh blood.

"Yes. I just…" She stood, nervously twisted her tissue in her hands.

"You're bleeding," he said, spotting the raw scrape on her knee.

"I fell," she said, blushing.

"You fell…" He frowned. Scarlet had always struck him as particularly graceful. "In your sneakers?"

She blushed an even brighter shade of pink. "I was running away and I tripped."

"Running away from what?"

"Sam Albright," she muttered. "After I punched him."

"Who is Sam Albright and why did he need punching?" Liam took a firm grip on his temper—Sam Albright was none of his business, but if he had hurt Scarlet, Liam thought he might make it his business.

"My date," she said. "He… put his hands where they were not invited to be."

"Ah," said Liam, swallowing down his fury, and smiling at Scarlet instead. He walked over to her desk and spotted the Band-Aids buried in the debris of the drawer. "Sit, please," he said, plucking one out of the box.

She dropped into her chair with a froth of petticoats. He knelt down, stripped the Band-Aid from its wrapper, and pressed it against her knee. His fingertips caressed her skin around the bandage, but he managed to stop them there.

"Does Sam need consent explained to him further?" He asked, staring up into her sea-blue eyes and forcing his hands to rest on the arms of the chair. Although, that wasn't much better than having them on her knee. Now his hands were within millimeters of her bare arms and wanted very badly to run an exploratory fingertip along the soft inner skin of her elbow.

"I don't know," said Scarlet, sniffing. "He grabbed me and

shoved his hand in my underwear and I cracked him in the jaw and ran. I know it was a date, but that wasn't... I didn't want..."

She looked miserable and Liam cocked his head to one side trying to figure out his next step, but he was having trouble thinking with the fluttering scent of her in his nostrils. He loved the way she smelled. Everyone else in the office reeked of perfumes and scents. Scarlet was one of the few who smelled like herself. And also a little bit like the woods on a spring day. It was intoxicating.

"I'm sorry," she said. "I don't mean to dump this on you. I came here because I knew I had Band-Aids and I live out in Bed-Stuy. I was just looking forward to having a stupid fun Halloween for once. My Mom never let us dress up as kids and I wanted..."

She smiled awkwardly.

"You wanted to be like everyone else," he said. "I understand. We never really did Halloween either. My parents... didn't like it," he finished lamely. How was he supposed to explain that Halloween felt like one mask too many?

"Everyone else makes it look easy," she said. "Sexy costumes and candy. I thought I could figure that out."

"You nailed the costume," he offered, realizing he was still kneeling between her knees and now that he had tilted his head, he could see her panties were ruffled as well.

"Thanks," she said brightening. "I couldn't do the high-heels. That seemed unsafe. Which, considering I tripped in Converse, was probably a smart move. Although, I don't think it was entirely my fault. I tripped over some electrical cables the haunted house place had taped to the floor. I don't think that was OSHA approved."

"Certainly not ADA compliant," he said, with a grin—only Scarlet would worry about whether the Occupational Safety and Hazard Administration had approved a haunted house. She blushed a little like she knew she was being silly. "Want to go get a drink?" he asked.

She blinked at him, her eyes still glossy with unshed tears. "Yes?"

"All right then Ms. Hood, give me a moment to collect my jacket and I'll be ready to lure you down the wrong path."

She chuckled. "Oh, good. I've always wanted to be lured."

Liam tried not to question his intentions as he pulled on his jacket. Some things were just instinct. He could worry about consequences later and God, did he need some sort of distraction. Between the full moon and the fact that he hadn't made it home for a hunt this month, he was starting to go a little bonkers.

She was waiting for him when he came out of the office, a tiny basket in her hands and a sweetly nervous expression on her face.

"You don't mind going out with me looking like this, do you?"

Liam contemplated that. Truly what he wanted was to stay in with her looking like that. But, no, going out with Scarlet looking like a wolf's wet dream wasn't going to be a problem.

"It's fine," he said with a shrug. "I don't think anyone will notice honestly. It's Halloween."

"That's true," she agreed. "And if anyone asks, we'll tell them you're the wolf."

"Yes," he agreed. "I am definitely the wolf."

"You know what I always wondered about Little Red Riding Hood?" she asked, as he led the way to the elevator.

"How anyone could mistake the wolf for the grandmother?" It was the part of the story that always made his family nervous. It was too blatantly close to the truth.

"No, I wonder where the wolf was going before he met Little Red. No one ever seems to wonder if she lured him off *his* path."

"Well, he's the bad guy," argued Liam, although he had to admit he liked her interpretation.

"Well, of course," said Scarlet. "The bad guy isn't going to tell you that she's the bad guy."

"What do you mean?" he asked with a frown.

"The wolf died. It's Little Red who lived to tell the story and craft the marketing message. For all we know, Little Red lured the wolf to the cottage to kill her grandmother and then had the huntsman kill the wolf."

"Little Red," said Liam, feeling more attracted to Scarlet with every word out of her mouth—her pretty red-tinted mouth with the invitingly soft lips. "Should I be worried for my safety?"

"My grandmother lives out of state. And I like wolves," she said giving him a saucy wink.

Liam grinned, showing all his teeth. "Then, perhaps I can interest you in this very dark little lane just off the beaten path." He gestured to the elevator as the doors slid open.

She chuckled again and Liam felt smug. She didn't laugh much during working hours.

"Actually," he said as they entered the elevator, "I was going to grab a drink at Maxim's in the upstairs bar. If you're up for that." He waited for her to be impressed. The private club above the dance hall at Maxim's was one of the cities hardest to get invitations. Of course, that was mostly because they had rather stringent restrictions on membership. Money was only half the requirement for getting through the door – members also had to be a Supernatural being of some kind. They'd relaxed their policy in the last decade though. Humans were now allowed with an escort.

"I've only lived here a few months," said Scarlet. "I don't know where, or what, anything is, so wherever you want to go." She looked embarrassed and standing in the closed space of the elevator Liam found her scent heady and drool-inducing. He wanted to lean in and lick her. She was so perfectly innocent that he thought he probably ought to feel guilty about all the things he was going to do to her.

But he didn't.

"Great," he said, forcing himself to keep his hands in his pockets and his tongue in his mouth for the moment. "I think you'll like Maxim's."

Tonight was going to be just what he needed.

EPISODE 2

MAXIM'S

Scarlet

Scarlet hadn't realized when Liam had said "the upstairs bar" that what he'd meant was *the private club that treats me like a king*. And even if she had known that she'd never have expected to be treated like a queen. She hadn't ever been to any place quite so decadent and she found that she did indeed like it. Of course, she liked everything right at the moment. She liked the dim, romantic lighting, the expensive cocktails. She liked the way the waitresses all had their faces painted in *Calavera* make-up, like Day of the Dead sugar skulls, and the band, playing sultry jazz, were dressed in the tattered finery of voodoo. But most of all she liked the way Liam Grayson's knee was rubbing up against hers and the way his arm draped over the back of the booth and almost around her shoulders.

She had the feeling that she shouldn't have said yes to his invitation. But co-workers were allowed to go out for drinks, weren't they? It wasn't her fault that Liam, who had always been rather brusque at the office, was turning out to be charming and easy to talk to. Scarlet had to admit that she was finding it harder and harder not to be *too* open with him. She probably shouldn't have let him order her the third cocktail.

She'd had a little bit of a crush on handsome, dark-haired Liam Grayson since the first time she'd seen him—he was so vibrantly *more* than everyone else at the office in a way she couldn't put her finger on, but that she found instantly attractive. That was why she'd volunteered to be his secretary. The other girls in the pool didn't

like him. They all agreed he was hot, but they said he was demanding and unfriendly. And one girl said he creeped her out and she
didn't like going into his office. But Scarlet didn't find him creepy,
weird, or demanding. Liam didn't seem to ask for anything unusual
at work. He just wanted things done right and so far, Scarlet hadn't
had any problems delivering. And now, after work, he was funny
and warm and had a growly rough tone to his voice and eyes the
color of whiskey, and all of that made Scarlet rather breathless.

Scarlet excused herself and went to the restroom. Coming out
of the stall, she was startled to see herself in the mirror. She hadn't
worn her hair in braids in years and the effect was to make her look
like her teenage self while the tight dress elevated her breasts to
a ridiculous degree and the short skirt, which was something she
would never have worn at any point in her life, made her look like
one of those pin-up cartoons of Little Red Riding Hood. She stared
at herself, uncertain what to think, ambivalent about her own overt
sexuality.

Scarlet wondered what her sister would say if she saw Scarlet's
costume. Azure was always, first and foremost, herself. She never
understood wanting to dress up as anyone else. Her brother Ochre
would probably just roll his eyes. With two sisters, he had a tenden-
cy to describe anything he didn't want to think about as *girly stuff* and
move on. But Liam had thought it was sexy. So had several others
in the bar. She pivoted, her skirt ruffling around the pale skin of
her thighs. She felt a little dirty in the costume and, although she
wasn't sure why she liked that. She pictured Liam doing what Sam
had done and she bit her lip. Liam's hands would not have been
unwelcome.

Abruptly she stopped smiling and went to wash her hands.
She needed to stop. Liam Grayson was strictly off-limits. He was

probably just being nice anyway. Taking pity on the lowly secretary who'd had a bad night.

A dark-haired woman came in, slamming through the door, a little unstable in her leopard print heels and skin-tight satin dress.

"Woah," she said taking in Scarlet. "You are so fucking hot."

Scarlet was surprised into letting out a laugh.

"No, seriously. Who are you taking home and can I come watch?"

"My boss. No. Maybe. And, no! You can't watch."

The woman laughed. "Bummer. But what's with the indecision?"

"He's my boss," wailed Scarlet, giving in to the sacrosanct holiness of the bathroom confessional. "I feel so bad, but I want him *so* much."

The woman laughed again, her dress seams creaking a little against the assault. "But honey," she said, "you didn't wear that outfit to be good."

Scarlet looked at herself in the mirror. "I wore it because I wanted to be... cool. Like all the TV show versions of Halloween. Only it turns out, I still feel like me."

"Yeah," said the woman, also looking at their reflections. "I used to feel that way. And then I realized one thing."

"What was that?" asked Scarlet, copying the arrogant tilt of the woman's head.

"I'm a fucking tiger."

"Sometimes, when no one is looking, I'm a badass motherfucker," said Scarlet. "But I don't know how to do it when someone's looking."

The tiger woman laughed again. "Oh my God, I love you and you smell so good. Now go out there, stick your tongue down his throat and let nature take care of the rest."

"I envy your confidence," said Scarlet. "But I worry about Monday morning."

"Fuck Monday morning."

"I will keep that in mind," said Scarlet. She smiled as she left, but the second the bathroom door swung shut her confidence wavered.

She went back out to the restaurant, hesitating by the dance floor, looking for an open path across to their table. What she really ought to do was go over and thank Liam for the lovely evening and then pour herself into a cab she couldn't really afford and head for home. But standing there on the edge of everything, she kept catching glimpses of him through the moving bodies. And every time she saw him, it was a little snapshot of something Scarlet wanted desperately. She wanted to feel the way he made her feel all the time—dangerously burning hot and perfectly safe all at the same time. And if she couldn't have it all the time would it really be so bad to have it just for one night?

"Hey there, Red," said an angular fellow, pulling away from his table full of rowdy friends to plant himself in front of her. "Come on over to our table. We'll show you a good time."

Scarlet stared into his hard, dark eyes and felt the brittle, metallic taste in her mouth that told her that he was not safe for her to be around. Her grandmother would not approve of Scarlet frequenting a place that served his kind of person, but there were a lot of *others* in the city. Scarlet thought it was speciesist to exclude certain types just because their eating habits were… predatory.

"No thanks," she said, smiling politely. "I'm with someone."

"Come on," he said stepping closer, filling her view. She refused to back up, trying hard to control the flutter of nerves in her stomach. She found her open-minded attitude not as easy to maintain in practice as it was in theory, and she wished she hadn't left her long, straight, wooden hair pin in her basket at the table. She didn't want to have to do anything overt here in front of everyone, but she would.

"Just one drink. Your date won't mind."

Then he smiled at her and Scarlet saw all of his teeth. All. Of. His. Teeth. Part of her was shocked that he would dare be so blatant in public. The other half felt pinned in place like a butterfly to a display board. She knew it was the vampire glamour that made their gaze hypnotic and that she'd made a mistake looking into those deadly eyes in the first place. But now that she was here, knowing what the mistake was didn't actually help her.

Scarlet swallowed hard, willing herself to speak up, say something, do anything.

Run.

EPISODE 3
DANCING

Scarlet

"Just one drink. Your date won't mind."

The words hung in the air, waiting for a response. Scarlet knew that she'd better give one because his hand was already reaching out to take possession of her wrist. He was dressed in a black suit of some slick-looking material over a black silk shirt. His hand against the black cuff of the suit was unnaturally pale and her guts squirmed at the idea of those cold fingers touching her skin.

"Yes, I will," said Liam. The man in front of her jumped, startled by Liam's words. He swung around to face Liam only to find that Liam was far closer than expected. Liam must have used the music to cover his approach because Scarlet hadn't heard him either.

The vampire made an odd jerking motion as if expecting Liam to make room, but the only move Liam made was to raise his eyebrows. The man had to edge off to one side to get out from between Scarlet and Liam. The maneuver was awkward and Scarlet tried not to smirk in amusement. Suddenly the vampire wasn't nearly as frightening as he had been a moment ago.

"This one's mine," said Liam.

"So close-minded," said one of the others at the table. They were all wearing various shades of black, like the first rule of vampire club was always wear slimming / threatening colors. Only the one who had spoken had been bold enough to wear something as garish as a color—a ruby red tie. She compared the entire table's ensembles to Liam's navy suit and found them wanting. Liam looked like he could tie all of them in knots. Did vampires only turn an-orexic male models?

The first man glanced over at the table and Scarlet flashed back to every encounter with every high-school bully ever. This one was so clearly currying favor with the others, puffing up to impress. Scarlet frowned. She hadn't had any patience with bullies in high school and she didn't have any now. She couldn't believe she'd let herself be swayed for one single moment by that jackass. She pulled herself up straight and prepared to deliver a piece of her mind.

"He's right," said the first man, trying to recover some of his bravado, inching forward and running a soft hand down Liam's arm. Scarlet's mouth swung open a little. She was fine with gay people. In the greater scheme of things to worry about, she could never understand why people worried about sexual orientation. But this was not gay, this was...

"You *both* could have fun with us."

Sex as a weapon.

She looked at Liam. Was this going to be a thing? Would he freak out like some sort of homophobic backwoods idiot that she'd gone to high school with? Had Scarlet been a betting woman, she would have bet the vampire was doing it strictly to mess with Liam's head. He *wanted* Liam to react, but Scarlet couldn't predict how Liam would respond. Liam let out an annoyed, rumbling sort of growl like he couldn't believe he was having to put up with this shit.

"I like pets," added the man with an overly toothy grin. Scarlet found it very sloppy to let the mask slip even so far. But apparently, it pushed Liam from irked into annoyed because he kneed the man in the balls. Scarlet wasn't sure she even saw him move, but she heard the impact.

"Ooh!" she squeaked her hands flying to her mouth in surprise as Liam followed the knee up with a punch to the jaw. No one at the vampire's table moved as their friend crashed to the floor. He rolled to his back, looking up at them in a dazed stupor. Scarlet was impressed. It was very difficult to stun a vampire and Liam had done it with ease.

Liam always looked fit under his suit, but for the first time, Scarlet noticed how thick his forearms were. And just how much tailoring must happen to make his suit jackets fit right across his shoulders. She knew she shouldn't be enthralled by such brawny displays, but she was learning a lot about herself this evening. From her own speciesist tendencies to the fact that watching Liam pummel vampires made her more than a little bit wet, Scarlet felt like this evening was going to take a lot of meditating on.

Later. When Liam wasn't looking at her like he wanted to lick her like a lollipop.

"As I said—this one is mine. Get your own." Liam held out his hand and Scarlet took it, reveling in the way the vampire looked both angry and defeated as Liam led her out onto the dance floor.

"Should we worry about them or call security or something?" asked Scarlet, trying to sneak a look over her shoulder at the table where the vampires were distinctly not looking their way.

"No," said Liam. "If it were a problem, security would have been here already and they wouldn't be talking to us. Those asshats should know better."

"Oh," said Scarlet. She didn't want to add anything else because she didn't want to admit that clubs of this caliber were entirely out of her experience. She felt like a country bumpkin or the kitchen maid who had somehow managed to get herself invited to dance with the prince. The gorgeous, beautiful prince with amber eyes who was holding her very tight and had just punched out a vampire for her.

"I don't think I like this skirt as much when we're dancing," he muttered, looking down at the offending garment. Scarlet was ambivalent on the subject because she knew that if it hadn't been for the mound of tulle and lace, she would have been plastered against his front and that probably wasn't what good girls did. But she wasn't feeling very good at the moment. She was feeling like she wanted to take the prince home and do very naughty things to him.

"Liam," she said, trying not to sound as breathless as she felt. "You didn't have to say you were my date."

"I didn't say I was your date. I said you were mine."

"Oh," said Scarlet, staring into Liam's warm brown eyes. She knew this was her moment to say that no, she didn't belong to him or anyone, thank him for the drinks and the punching and then go home. She opened her mouth to say that, or at least say something, when another couple jostled into them. Scarlet clung closer to Liam, losing all pretense of proper dance form, her arms sliding around his neck. He dipped his head down and let his lips drag across her neck, before taking her earlobe gently in his mouth. His breath was hot and wet and his tongue flicked out, running along the crest of her ear. She let out an involuntary gasp and her knees seemed to have suddenly turned to jelly.

"Time to go, Little Red," he whispered.

"Yes, Wolf," she replied.

EPISODE 4
Liam's Apartment

Liam

Liam gently tugged the little puff of a sleeve down off her shoulder while his tongue traced the top swell of Scarlet's breast. She let out a moan and he ran his hand down her back pulling the zipper with it. She wasn't wearing a bra. The costume had been doing all the support work and when he pulled the other sleeve down it left her topless in a frothing pool of netting and lace. He pulled away and Scarlet made a panicked noise that stroked his ego more than any compliment.

He kissed her while he finished stripping out of his shirt and pants. The cab ride home from Maxim's had tested his self-control on so many levels. He knew the cabbie had noticed the way Liam kept a possessive hand on her thigh the entire ride, but he had been struggling to keep his claws from growing—letting go of her hadn't really been an option. The scent of Scarlet had become richer as they drove, filling his nostrils and pushing his instinctual self to the forefront. And when they had reached his apartment he hadn't bothered with words—he wasn't sure he could have. He simply pulled her into his bedroom.

Not that she had protested. The only time she had objected to anything was when he'd stopped touching her. That was fine with him. He planned on touching, tasting, and fucking her for the rest of the damn night.

He pushed Scarlet back onto the bed and removed the ruffle-covered panties. Then he dove beneath the froth, testing, exploring, and tasting, allowing her to fill up every sense. Knowing that the skirt would cover any irregularities, he let the mask slide a little. His teeth became longer and his tongue wider, stronger, and more agile.

Scarlet moaned, her legs quaking, her hands buried in his fu… hair. Her taste was intoxicating as he wrapped his tongue around her clit.

"Wolf! Wolf! Oh God, Wolf!"

She was writhing underneath his tongue and he reveled in the control he had of her body. He slowed down, making her wait, teasing his tongue inside her and then out to flick up to her clit. She was panting and shaking, her hands locked in his hair.

"Wolf, please! Please, Wolf!"

Beneath her skirt he grinned and lapped her entire pussy, spreading his tongue wide to take in everything. Once he had satisfied himself, he gave her what she wanted. Concentrating on her clit, she came moments later. He carefully made sure his face was appropriate and stood up.

He stripped her dress off and pulled on a condom.

"Turn over," he commanded.

"Yes, Wolf," she gasped, still breathless, and crawled onto the center of his bed on all fours. The sight of her there, round ass and sweet little pussy in the air, swaying back and forth a little, waiting for him, made him achingly hard.

He mounted her and took her with hard, driving thrusts, claiming her inside and out. Wanting nothing more than to own her entirely.

She screamed his name, her hands clenching the sheets into her fists. He gave her a moment and then continued until she was moaning and panting again.

"Wolf! Wolf! Please, Wolf! More!"

Her voice was strained and high, begging him to do what he wanted to do anyway. He couldn't remember the last time someone had made him want to fuck her in all of his shapes. He could feel the hackles rising along his spine as he got closer to coming. He knew he probably ought to back off and be a little softer. Humans didn't always like what he liked.

"God, yes, Wolf, harder!"

She arched and begged, submitting to him utterly and he growled in approval.

He leaned into her, seizing her by the shoulder, as he thrust and nipped her on the back of the neck. She came in a hard jerk, clenching around him so hard that he came too and they collapsed onto the sheets.

Scarlet

Scarlet roused herself from a half-dream state and tried to pry herself out from under Liam. He growled as she clumsily exited the bed, her arms, and legs not quite answering her commands.

"Bathroom," she said, in response to his complaint, and he subsided back onto the pillows.

She staggered into the bathroom and clutched at the sink. Her braids had a nimbus of small loose hairs and one had become half unraveled. Her lips were swollen from kissing and her mascara had smeared down her face. She swiped at her cheeks with a piece of toilet paper; trying to look a little less like she'd just been fucked so good that she'd cried.

Scarlet took a deep breath and let it out again. She had fucked Liam Grayson. She had fucked the boss. She was in such deep shit if anyone ever found out. It was never the boss who got fired in these situations. There were so many red flags on this entire evening. He was her boss. He had said she belonged to him and he'd certainly acted like he owned every inch of her. She bit her lip remembering the feeling of his lips, his tongue, his hands, and how it felt to have him inside of her. She couldn't help thinking that if belonging to him meant she could have him whenever she wanted… No. She shook her head. It was ridiculous—she was a modern woman—she didn't believe in that kind of thing. She should be offended. She shouldn't like that… right? That was bad? Except she didn't feel bad. She felt like she'd just had the best sex of her entire life.

She looked at the door to the bedroom and tried to figure out her next move.

Go back in there and suck his dick until she made him as crazed as he had made her.

No. She should be sensible. She should…

Wrap her legs around him. Fuck him until the only word he remembered was her name.

Scarlet moaned. Liam Grayson was so far out of her league that she'd never even considered what to do in this situation. Why should she? Liam Grayson had never looked twice at her. Only Liam Grayson was not the same as her wild wolf. Wolf not only looked but tasted, claimed, owned. She had never experienced anything close to the pleasure of Wolf's touch. She didn't know what she was supposed to do, but she was certain she wanted that pleasure again.

She looked at herself in the mirror.

"You are a very bad girl, Little Red," she said. Her mirror self simply looked smugly wicked.

"Right," she agreed. "I guess we are definitely stepping off the path."

Scarlet finished cleaning up, then went back out to the bedroom and crawled into bed with her boss.

Liam

Liam drifted into wakefulness. He was face down in the pillows, one arm stretched over Scarlet. She looked angelic in her sleep with her blonde hair still rippled from her braids spread across the pillow. He'd unwound them while she'd been going down on him, wanting to run his fingers through the heavy golden strands. Her mouth had been like velvet and her hair like silk as it brushed up against his thighs.

Liam sat up, stretched, and padded into the kitchen. He pulled open the fridge and glanced over his shoulder. Scarlet was still sound asleep, so he reached into the Tupperware and pulled out a handful of raw venison. Chewing, he grabbed the glass bottle of milk and put it on the counter. His phone chirped as he reached for a glass.

HEY! YOU'RE COMING HOME FOR THANKSGIVING RIGHT? MOM'S TWEAKING.

Liam sighed at his younger brother's text. When was their mother *not* tweaking? Aisling Grayson hated that he was living in the city. It had been beneficial to the pack, but she still hated it. Ever since his father's death, she had been reluctant to let any of the pack go more than fifty miles away. He kept thinking she would lighten up, but it wasn't getting better. And the last few months had been one last-minute deadline after another—he hadn't made it home nearly as often as he intended. But now that he had Scarlet—he grinned at his double entendre—work was finally lightening up. Going home for the holiday would be the easiest way to smooth things over with Aisling, but her piss poor mood made it hard to want to.

YEAH. TELL MOM I'M COMING FOR THE ENTIRE WEEK. AND

I MIGHT BE ABLE TO SNEAK OUT FOR AN EXTRA WEEKEND BEFORE
THEN TOO.

THAT WOULD BE AWESOME!

Paxton's text sounded genuinely excited and Liam felt guilty.
He was avoiding his mother, not everyone else. He did need to go
home, but he got tired of arguing with Aisling.

There was a rustle of movement from the bed and he snuck a
peek through the bedroom door. Scarlet had turned over onto her
side, leaving a ribbon of gold hair across the pillow. He grabbed
another hunk of meat and considered his next move. Ordinarily, he
tried to usher his human distractions out the door shortly after he
woke up. He didn't need the smell of them all over his things. But
he liked how Scarlet smelled.

He had barely finished his snack when he heard Scarlet yawn
and then the rustle of sheets and fabric. He quickly gulped down the
rest of his venison and washed his hands. He was properly drinking
his milk from a glass, like a civilized human being, when Scarlet
came out of the bedroom.

She was clutching her dress in one hand and seemed to be looking for her socks. He'd flung them somewhere. He really couldn't
remember where.

"I'm going to have to get a cab," she said, finding the sock
on the floor outside of the bedroom door. She added an awkward
laugh, her cheeks flushing a light pink. He raised an eyebrow and
made an inquiring noise.

"I really can't do the walk of shame for an entire subway ride
home to Brooklyn. The costume makes it so obvious."

He grunted. He was not pleased with the idea of her leaving.

"No," he said, finishing his swallow of milk. "I will drive you.
At some point. Tomorrow."

That seemed far enough away. He could spend the weekend

fucking her and figure out where to go with things on Monday. She was holding the dress in front of her and her nipples were cresting the foam of netting. They looked delectable, but she shifted uncomfortably.

"Liam…"

The noise he made in response to the use of his proper name wasn't entirely human.

"No," she said, straightening up. "No, it has to be said."

He stared at her, waiting for her important words, embarrassed that he hadn't been able to use his own.

"We are not supposed to be doing this."

"According to who?" he asked.

"According to our employer," she said impatiently. "So, I think this had better be…" she seemed to flounder for words, "just a weekend fling."

He restrained himself from growling his disagreement. Although he'd just placed his own similar limit on their time together, hearing her say that there would be a time in which she would not be in his bed angered him. She belonged to him.

"Is that what you want?" he asked, trying to keep emotions out of his voice.

She opened her mouth and he nearly laughed. Her entire body said more clearly than any words that it was not what she wanted. "Yes," she lied, bringing her chin up, trying to look firm. It was an utter failure.

"Whatever you want," he said.

"All right," she said, with a nod.

He set the glass in the sink and came around the counter to her. He took the dress from her hand and dropped it on the floor. "But it's only Saturday, so for now we do what I want."

"Yes, Wolf," she said.

EPISODE 5

MONDAY

Scarlet

Scarlet put her hand to her chest, trying to still the nervous flutter of butterflies that swirled across her entire body. She had made it through half of Monday without being alone with Liam. He had driven her back to her apartment after midnight the previous night and she had slept fitfully until the cold fall sunlight had crept through the window.

She'd ended up going for a run before work, wanting desperately for the fresh air to clear her head. Instead, she had come home more confused than ever. It wasn't like she'd never had sex before. She'd had three boyfriends. And she'd had two whole drunken hookups upon arriving in the city. But those had made her feel gunky and gross. She'd moved to the city to concentrate on her career, not on boys or living the magical lifestyle of *Friends*. Not that her career was going especially well. She had graduated with honors from a well-respected MBA program and arrived in the city only to discover that the rent was due and that everyone had an MBA. So she'd swallowed her pride, dumbed-down her resume, and taken a job as a secretary. So far it had worked out in her favor. In the two months that she'd been working at Fosters Financial, she'd heard about three positions before they hit the job boards. She'd had one call back and one interview. Neither had been quite right, but she was certain that she could get a non-secretarial job soon.

And then she could date Liam.

Scarlet groaned and tried to resist the urge to bang her head on her desk. Liam was not the goal. A career was the goal. Changing the world was the goal. And also making her family eat their words a little. She was tired of being treated like she was naïve and delusional for her career choice. If she told her sister that she was dating someone in the financial industry, Azure would call her a total sellout. It was bad enough her family already thought it, but if she came home with a big city boyfriend they would say it out loud. And besides, when she'd said their fling, or whatever it had been, was only for the weekend, Liam hadn't objected even a little bit. So really, this was going nowhere and she needed to pull herself together.

Of course, neither of them had done very much talking over the weekend. Liam Grayson probably screwed every secretary that crossed his path. He was very good at it. He'd obviously had lots of practice. And this morning at all the meetings he'd barely even looked at her. So... clearly limiting it to the weekend had been the right decision. She would just have to hold her head high, do the job, and hope that the latest resume she'd turned in would be her ticket out of here.

Scarlet took a deep breath, smoothed her skirt, and took the reports she'd completed into Liam's office. She could hear him down the hall talking to Brett Hubbard. Liam's voice had a distinctive bass note that she could always identify, even from the hallway. She started to lay out the reports and her notepad on his desk, mentally rehearsing her talking points.

"I finished the Hearseman comparison," she said, not looking up when he came in.

"That's good," he said shutting the door. She tried to ignore the wonderful closeness to him as he crossed the room to her.

"I wasn't sure if—"

She cut off with a little gasp as he ran his tongue over her neck.

"Wolf," she quavered as he nibbled her ear. His hands were

working her skirt up and soon they were on the bare flesh of her thighs. His fingers ran over the lace of her panties. She moaned and nestled against him, rubbing her ass against his cock. One hand continued to caress her through her panties while the other went to her throat, turning her head so that he could capture her mouth with his.

"Wolf," she tried to separate herself from him, but only managed to move her mouth. He had her pinned against the desk. "Wolf, we said the weekend." Her voice ended on a squeak as his fingers slid beneath the edge of her panties.

"Yes," he murmured, "but I lied."

He was stroking her clit with firm fingers and she was so wet she knew he could tell she wanted him.

"We can't," she gasped, wriggling against him. She could feel his hard cock pressing up against her and she longed to have it inside her.

"Yes, we can." He didn't sound worried or argumentative. He sounded as calm as if he were talking about the weather.

Abruptly, he withdrew his hand and Scarlet heard herself make a little yip of protest. He spun her around and pushed her onto the desk. Before she had even registered what he was doing, he had peeled off her panties and dropped them on the floor. His hand went back to her pussy and this time he slid two fingers inside her while his thumb rubbed her swollen clit. He ran nuzzling, hot kisses along her neck. She clung to the edge of the desk as her legs spread involuntarily for him.

"We're going to get caught," she moaned, arching as he stroked her just right.

He moved up to her mouth, kissing her fiercely, but then pulled away and cocked his head at the door.

"Oh. Yeah. Actually, we are. Brett's on his way in."

He grabbed her by the hips and set her back on her feet, pushing her skirt down.

She hurried to re-tuck her blouse, trying to smooth herself into some semblance of professional appearance. She spotted her underwear on the floor, but Liam was faster.

"Nope. These are mine now."

He pocketed the panties and moved to sit behind his desk as a sharp knock rapped on the door.

"Come in!" he called, before turning to Scarlet as if they'd been talking the entire time. "I'll go over the Hearseman report first. Hey, Brett. But I think we might need to run a few more comparables. Can you do a database search and find me some more companies about that size?"

Scarlet nodded mutely and picked up her notepad. Hurrying toward the door, hoping that it didn't look like an abject retreat.

She sat down at her desk, trying not to gulp air like she'd been running. She recognized that she was not an expert in romantic affairs, but she had thought she at least understood the basics of dating. The only problem was that nothing about Liam was basic.

She logged into her computer, hoping that the rattle of keys would make it at least sound like she was working.

Had he ever had any intention of sticking to the weekend rule?

Liam

Liam waited until the door was firmly closed and he heard Brett's off-key whistling head down the hall before he took Scarlet's panties out of his pocket and held them to his face. She smelled so good. Like spring. Like the earth right after the first drops of rain hit the soil.

On the way to work, he'd toyed with the idea of following her stupid weekend fling rule. And then he'd stepped off the elevator and caught the first wafting scent of her. By the time he'd glimpsed her chatting with one of the other secretaries in the break room, he'd known that he was nowhere near done with Scarlet.

Liam tucked her underwear back in his pocket with a smile and reached for her Hearseman report, amused that she was being so conscientious. He felt like the weekend had earned them some slacking. He certainly hadn't managed to do much more than respond to a few emails all morning. Honestly, after the endurance marathon of sex, all he wanted to do was curl up with Scarlet for a nap. But she either had more energy than he did or felt required to double down on her professionalism, which was adorable. Hell, she was adorable. Every time she said *Yes, Wolf,* he wanted to... do everything he'd been doing to her all weekend.

He flipped open the report and then realized there were at least five more pages. Slowly he read through it. She had included everything that he'd intended to do once she pulled the initial data.

He scratched his head. That wasn't normal for a secretary. He thought he'd been pushing his luck to have her pull the data, but she seemed so smart and hadn't been confused when he'd asked for it. None of the secretaries Fosters Financial hired ever seemed to know the first thing about what Fosters Financial actually did. Apparently, he'd hit the jackpot in more ways than one.

The door opened and Scarlet came in her notepad clutched in one hand and a resolute expression on her face. She carefully shut the door and planted herself in front of his desk and held out her hand.

"My underwear, please."

He couldn't stop the grin from spreading across his face. Firm Scarlet was priceless.

"No."

"Yes!" She added a little foot stomp that made him wish she was wearing her Little Red costume so he could watch everything bounce.

"If you want them back you have to come over tonight."

"No! This is strictly against company policy and I need the job."

"Yes, very against the rules," he agreed, getting up and going around to her side of the desk. "Fortunately, you're a rebel."

She bit her lip and then he did the same, leaning in to kiss along her bottom lip with tiny nibbles. She softened for a moment and then sprang backward.

"No, no I'm not. I'm a rule follower. Just one of the herd, coloring inside the lines—that's me! Completely normal."

This time he did laugh, even as he reached out and pulled her to him. He kissed her gently and softly, luring her into relaxing against him.

"Wolf," she sighed, in the weakest of protests.

"My Little Red," he whispered, "normal people don't have to say they're normal."

Her eyes flew open and she stared at him, clearly uncertain of how to respond.

"You will come over tonight," he said. "It's what you want to do anyway and think how much easier it will be to argue with me when there's no one else around."

She looked annoyed but didn't have a comeback, so he kissed her again.

"The Hearseman report was awesome, by the way. You saved me a ton of time. Can you do the same thing with the Applecourt account?"

"Yes?" She looked off-balance and he had every intention of keeping her that way.

"Great."

She glared at him. "Liam," she said, using his name like a weapon, "you are too used to getting your own way."

"Come over tonight and you can have your way with me," he offered and she gave a halfway decent growl before stomping out of the office.

EPISODE 6

THANKSGIVING

Scarlet

Scarlet stared at Liam's white plaster ceiling. He lived in a small, but very expensive apartment on the edge of Central Park. In a few minutes, her alarm would go off and Liam would wake up and blink at her like he couldn't remember who she was, and then he would smile and kiss her. It was how her mornings started now. It had been three weeks and she'd spent most of the nights at Liam's apartment. They sometimes went to Maxim's or ordered dinner in, but the night's all ended the same, with her sweaty and delirious from pleasure and wrapped in her wolf's arms. Then they would wake up and Scarlet would leave by herself so that they would arrive at the office at different times.

This morning would be different though. This morning they would leave together and go to the train station before parting for the Thanksgiving holiday. She knew he thought she was going home although she had carefully never said that. And she knew he was going to his family's property. Not that he ever specified exactly where that was. The amount of personal information he'd shared could be included in a tweet. She tried not to let that bother her. Just like she tried to not let it bother her that he never clarified how he viewed their relationship. He never said they were dating. He never said anything about going public. And the rest of his non-verbal signals weren't any more positive. Nothing said *not serious* quite like having to pack her toothbrush and a change of clothes every night of the week. He didn't even seem bothered by their arrangement.

Scarlet couldn't say that she felt the same. She had enough secrets in her life. She wasn't sure she wanted her relationship to be one of them. But every time she thought about bringing it up, he'd fuck the thought out of her head.

But her alarm was about to go off and then he would smile at her and kiss her and somehow that meant everything.

Liam's alarm rang five minutes before hers, startling her so that she jerked in surprise. Liam laughed at her and gathered her into his arms, spooning tightly against her, snuggling his face into the crook of her neck. He inhaled, running his mouth along her neck as if smelling and tasting her at the same time and Scarlet melted, breathing out and letting her silent morning angst go. It was hard to hold onto worry when he was hanging on to her.

They moved around each other in the silent dance of getting ready. Scarlet eating avocado toast over the sink and Liam carrying a glass of milk everywhere with him while he finished packing. She appreciated that he got his milk from a local dairy that was known to her family. It meant that she could have milk too. She tried not to wave her semi-vegetarianism around like a flag. It wasn't that she didn't like meat—the chemicals of the modern age made her a little crazy. And also itchy. All the radio waves were bad enough. Cable TV had been an absolute blessing for her family. Sending everything through cables made the air so much quieter. Everything still buzzed with electricity and radio and Wi-Fi and satellite signals and all the other rasping vibrating messages that had driven her mom to leave, and it wasn't as though Scarlet didn't feel it. Every morning she spent a few minutes hiding in the bathroom to complete her cleansing spells that allowed her to make it through her day. But some days the spells she used wouldn't cut it in this busy city and she had to take about eight of her migraine pills plus drive out to someplace with fewer signals in the air. But Scarlet still felt like it was worth it, particularly when she got to walk through the train station holding Liam's hand.

Saying goodbye was odd and Scarlet spent most of the trip trying to figure out why. As the train pulled into the station and she spotted her brother's pale blond head surveying the platform, looking for her, Scarlet realized that it was because Liam hadn't looked back. He'd kissed her goodbye and left to make his own train. The thought sat like a lump in her throat, but she swallowed it and went to the exit.

"Ochre!" she called, stepping out onto the platform and waving. Ochre Lucas lifted his head at the sound of his name, spotted her, and waved back.

"Hey!" he exclaimed striding toward her. He was close to six-foot-five and towered over most people. He swept her into a quick hug and set her back down again. "Ready to go?"

"Yeah," agreed Scarlet, hefting her backpack onto her shoulder and smiling at her brother. His hair, a little more red-gold than hers, was getting long again. He was the worst at remembering to get a haircut. She remembered when they'd been children, it had grown down his back because, after the first disastrous cut from Azure, he'd refused to let her try again. But he had been willing to let Scarlet braid it, which she had enjoyed enormously. Privately, Scarlet thought his long hair and pointed ears made him look like their father, but Scarlet had only met him the one time and she didn't like to ask Azure if her impression was right. When their grandmother had found them, she'd made Ochre get his hair cut. She said they needed to blend in. Diana had been right, and living with her had certainly been better than the subsistence life the Lucas siblings had been eking out on their own, but Scarlet found that she sometimes missed their wild-child days.

"Don't need to stop for any last-second supplies?" Ochre asked.

"I probably won't even need the ones I brought, will I?" asked Scarlet, looking up at Ochre in confusion.

"No," he said with a chuckle. "But you're all citified now. I thought you might be high-maintenance or something."

"I'm not sure how having a job that *doesn't* require me to sit in the dirt makes me high-maintenance, but OK." Scarlet rolled her eyes and Ochre laughed again. Sometimes being the youngest sibling sucked.

Ochre led the way out of the train station and out to the parking lot. She was used to following Ochre. His height made him easy to keep track of. Scarlet wondered if he ever got tired of being used as a signpost by his family and acquaintances. He never said anything, but he had always been the quiet one of the three of them.

"Hey, did you bring my bow?" asked Scarlet, climbing into the truck and noticing the lack of equipment.

"Ohhhhhh." Ochre grimaced and Scarlet sighed. "Sorry," said Ochre. "I forgot."

"It's OK," said Scarlet. So much for getting any meat on this trip. She had the distinct impression that this weekend was not going to go well.

They drove in until they were bumping down a logging road into the backcountry. Azure met them at Ochre's campsite. Azure was always the odd duck in the family. Although she was lanky like Ochre, and pale like Scarlet, and she shared the family blue eyes, she took after their father with thick black hair. She dressed in the witch tradition of all black—although Scarlet wasn't sure an outfit counted as witchy when it was dusty, faded, black jeans and a black zip-up hoodie.

"Scarlet!" Azure said holding out her arms. Scarlet hugged her and tried not to feel self-conscious that all of her clothes were newer than Azure's.

"I wasn't sure you'd come," said Azure, tucking a stray strand of hair behind Scarlet's ear. She had always been motherly. When they had been children it had been reassuring because their mother hadn't been able to be the kind of mom who tucked them in and read them stories. And after her mother had left, abandoning all of them, thirteen-year-old Azure had been the one who took care of them. It had been another two years before Diana had found them and brought them back to Virginia. And Scarlet appreciated that Azure had taken care of the family when they were younger, but these days Scarlet found her mother-knows-best attitude condescending. Scarlet was a grown adult, paying her own bills, living her own life. When was Azure going to stop telling her what to do?

"What part about *I'll be there* was unclear?" asked Scarlet with a tight smile.

"I just couldn't see it happening," said Azure with what felt like a fake smile—Scarlet tried not to give a wolf-like growl.

"What's the plan, Azure?" asked Ochre, going to the fire and giving it a poke. The embers flared up as he tossed in a fresh log.

"I have seen that the security forces the logging company hired will be here tomorrow. I have also seen that this is our moment of opportunity. We have a chance to change the course of events here, but I need both of you in order to accomplish it."

Azure looked from Scarlet to Ochre as if assessing how useful they were going to be. Scarlet was willing to bet Azure was no end of annoyed at needing them to get the job done.

"You want to do the thing we did in Richmond?" asked Ochre.

"Yes," said Azure, confidently. "I've made some refinements to the spell. I think we can do this. The problem is that we have to stay near the trees to make it work. And with the security forces coming in soon, there is some risk."

"I have to be at work on Monday," said Scarlet, frowning. As usual, Azure hadn't told them everything that was going on.

"Yes, your vitally important work as a secretary," said Azure. "How's that going?"

Scarlet took a deep breath.

"Hey," said Ochre, gently. "We all have our paths."

"Some paths are more worthwhile than others," snapped Azure. "I happen to think that saving old-growth forests are more important than going to work on Monday, but that's just me." Azure was still pissed at Scarlet for moving to the city and apparently wasn't going to be letting it go anytime soon. "Fortunately," Azure said, turning to Scarlet with a brittle smile, "I have seen that win or lose, we'll be done by Sunday night."

Scarlet took another deep breath and thought about leaving, but that would only make Azure believe she was right.

"I would have thought," said Scarlet, "that with the second sight you could see outside of your own ass, but apparently not."

Ochre coughed on a laugh and Azure's sapphire blue eyes narrowed in annoyance.

"Sunday night will be fine," Scarlet continued before Azure could speak. "What do you want to do?"

"The main protest will begin around noon. I want to be chained to the tree by Saturday. I think we'll begin the spell on Sunday morning, but I can't see that clearly. I think we're going to have to play it by ear. The security forces will try to stop us, but my people will protect us. If we can complete the spell, we will change the will of the people and the logging company will be stopped."

"And if we don't complete it, we'll get arrested or have the shit kicked out of us?" asked Scarlet.

"That may happen either way," said Azure. "I can't tell. That isn't a problem, is it?" she asked sweetly.

"Yes, it is. I'm sorry that I'm not an environmental activist or climatologist where everyone gives you the thumbs up and contributes to your bail go-fund-me."

Ochre chuckled at her description of their jobs.

"But I have a job where people care if I have a criminal record and they notice if I come back a beat-up mess. So, it would be really great if either of those things did *not* happen this weekend."

"The activists I work with will protect us as long as possible," said Azure. "But I can't guarantee it. If you're going to back out, now would be the time."

"You can't complete the spell without me," said Scarlet.

"And believe me, I'm working to fix that," said Azure, "but for now that's true."

"I said I was doing this and I'm doing this," said Scarlet. "But maybe you could work on not being a bitch the entire time we're chained to a tree."

"I wouldn't count on it," said Ochre. "You know bitch cakes are Azure's specialty."

"Excuse me!" snapped Azure, rounding on Ochre.

"Oh, what?" demanded Ochre. "You can play serene witch of the North to your little protest pals all you want, but Scarlet and I know what happens when you PMS. And speaking of which, do you want some chocolate or anything because it kind of seems like the red tide is flowing."

"That is just like a man! You blame everything on hormones."

"Well, it's either that or believe you're just a bitch," said Scarlet. "I said I'd be here and I'm here. Stop busting my hump."

"Speaking of hump-busting," said Ochre, poking at the fire some more. "Did anyone else get a ration of shit from Grandma over this?"

"Yeah," said Azure, looking gloomy and Scarlet wanted to hug her. "She said it was too obvious."

"Do we think she's right?" asked Ochre, looking between his sisters. They all valued their grandmother's judgment and Scarlet knew it troubled Azure and Ochre not to have her support.

"Maybe," said Scarlet, "but the Earth is dying. Do we really have the luxury of being discrete anymore?" Azure smiled at her and Scarlet smiled back.

"No," said Azure. "I don't think we do."

EPISODE 7

TRYPTOPHAN COMA

Liam

Liam left the pack and walked out to the bluff where he could stare at the moon. The family had celebrated Thanksgiving with the usual tradition of hunting wild turkeys. Feathers still floated in the air and everyone had settled into furry lumps under the pine trees. The pack was snuggled together, sharing their heat. It was usually his favorite part of visiting home. But tonight he couldn't sleep.

His mother had been predictably pissy even though he'd arrived earlier than expected. Nothing he did was ever good enough for Aisling anymore. Not since his father had died. Callum Grayson had been a multi-war military veteran. He'd retire and then re-enlist after a few decades, taking many of the younger pack members with him. It had been good discipline and experience, and the military rhythm of life had been good for the pack. But when Liam was still in high school, Callum had looked him in the eye and told him not to go into the military. Liam had been surprised. He had always assumed that he'd do the military thing at some point, but his father had simply said that he didn't think Liam would like it—there were too many orders. At first, Liam had been pissed and tempted to enlist just to spite him. He could take orders. Did his father think he was undisciplined or that he couldn't fight? Callum had demurred. He said Liam was a pathfinder, an experimentalist, and a thinker. He said the military needed those things, but he thought it would take Liam too long to get to a place where he could use all those skills freely. Meanwhile, the pack could use them immediately. In the end, Liam had accepted his father's mandate to stay home. But when Callum had died in an IED explosion planted by an ISIS warlock, Liam had questioned the decision all over again. And now he sometimes wondered if his mother questioned it too. If Liam had been there, could he have saved his father? Would they both have died? The questions hung in the air between them like ghosts that never quite materialized. He kept thinking that one or the other of them would ask the questions, but they never did. She just kept snapping at him and he kept taking it, but he could feel his patience for her grief wearing out and that made him feel even worse.

The moon was three-quarters full and fat, like a yellow ball of butter behind the lazily drifting shreds of clouds. The misty clouds gave the moon a pale rainbow corona and Liam sat down on a rock and fought the urge to howl. He wasn't a pup anymore. He could resist the pull of the moon. He just didn't like to admit how difficult it was.

He wondered what Scarlet was doing. Probably enjoying stuffing and pumpkin pie. He wondered what it would be like to have a Thanksgiving like that. He'd wanted to have the normal American Thanksgiving when he was a kid. His aunt had made him cranberry sauce one year. It had been delicious, but then his brother had accidentally put a paw in the bowl, red glop splattering everywhere. It had only looked mildly less violent than their actual meal.

He wondered how horrified Scarlet would be at his family's feast. He was trying not to let it bother him that she was vegetarian, but he couldn't deny that it got under his skin. Not that she ever commented when he ordered a steak at Maxim's or grilled up a sausage at home. She never commented on anything he did. It bugged him that she didn't take an interest. Yeah, he got it, she wasn't interested in commitment, the stupid job came first. But she spent all of her nights with him. Would it kill her to ask about something important? Not that they didn't talk about other things. His favorite conversations with her usually came directly after she'd read some sort of economics article and started with, "Now this is an interesting supposition." But while arguing about economics, psychology, the environment, and the intersectionality of racism and religion made for great dinner conversation, it left him feeling like he was missing a level of connection that he craved from not being with the pack.

He sighed. It might not kill her to ask, but it was definitely dangerous for him to answer. The fact that Scarlet didn't want to look too closely at his life was for the best. Why did he want to push his luck? He knew he probably ought to give it up. It wasn't like he could ever bring Scarlet home to the pack. His mother was never going to find a human acceptable. The marching orders were clear—there needed to be grand-pups. It was bad enough that he was living and working in the city. If he came home with a human, she would kick him out of the pack. So, really, the relationship was over before it even started. And after all, she was *just* a human. It wasn't like she was important.

Except that Liam had walked Scarlet to the train, put her on it, then turned and left, intending to prove to himself that he could take or leave her as he pleased. But instead of being easy, walking away had gotten harder with each step as he fought the instinct to go back and drag her home with him. He didn't understand what was wrong. He'd never gotten this hung up on anyone before. He should have taken Scarlet's edict of weekend fling more seriously. But every night he lay down with Scarlet, she would snuggle against him, fall asleep in his arms, and the sound of her breathing was like wind in the trees, lulling him to sleep.

"Hey," said Paxton, coming out of the trees. He was wearing a heavy sheepskin robe and carrying a second robe that Liam assumed was for him. Liam concentrated, furrowing his brow and trying to remember what a human shape felt like. His bones snapped and tendons stretched, his fur either poofed off or shrank back into his follicles. He shook his head and tried to breathe through the sharp, searing pain that accompanied every transformation. The pain dissipated almost immediately, but it was always a part of his life.

"Hey," Liam said, standing up and taking the robe from his brother. He wrapped it around himself and sat back down.

"Problems?" asked Paxton, sitting down next to him and taking in the moon.

"No," said Liam, surprised.

"Then why are you out here instead of in the communal tryptophan coma?"

"Couldn't sleep," said Liam with a shrug.

"You couldn't sleep last night either," said Paxton.

"Too much moon, I guess," said Liam. "Dunno."

"You're not becoming one of those stressed-out city people who need drugs to sleep, are you?" asked Paxton, his tone teasing.

"I usually sleep fine," said Liam, ignoring the little voice reminding him that usually, he had Scarlet. "I'll go lie down again in a bit when the moon moves."

Paxton was silent and after a moment it occurred to Liam to find Paxton's wakefulness suspicious.

"Do you have problems?" he asked.

"No!" said Paxton too swiftly.

"Want to try again?"

Paxton sighed. "It's not a problem exactly. It's just that…"

"That what?"

"You're in the city. It takes you too long to get here."

"Too long for what?" asked Liam. "Have I missed something?"

"Well, the meet and greets," began Paxton hesitantly.

"Oh, for fucks sake! I already talked to Mom about this. Don't tell me she's pestering you about it."

"What do you mean you already talked to Mom?" asked Paxton.

"The only reason me greeting visiting pack members is ever a problem is because wolves can't fucking use phones."

Paxton let out a bark of laughter.

"If visiting pack delegates could, I don't know, give us a call, send a calendar invite, flash some Morse code, whatever, then it wouldn't be such a scramble when they arrive. And if someone in our pack could pick up a damn phone and call me, I could be here on time. And, plus, it's not like visitors come directly here. They come to the airport and train station like everyone else. I'm closer to most visitors than you are. But again, no one ever fucking calls me until it's too late."

Paxton sighed. "It's Mom. She's the one who takes the calls and you know how anti-technology she is. And lately, I swear she's worse. It's all the recent warlock activity. She's twigging."

Liam nodded. Aisling's control-freak tendencies had soared after Callum's death. Liam thought it was unfortunate she didn't believe in human inventions, because she could really use some therapy.

"What recent warlock activity?" he asked, searching his memory, trying to recall any recent reports. Usually, he knew about warlocks before she did.

"I don't know. She talked to Aunt Bryn."

Liam groaned and Paxton laughed but kept going. "Someone says they smelled one a few weeks ago."

"Someone always says they smelled one," said Liam sourly. "I spent half my college years chasing these rumors. Once I figured out that warlocks smell like really shit-skunky weed and that no one in Mom's generation ever smoked pot, things got a lot clearer."

Paxton snort laughed so hard that he almost fell over.

"You didn't know that?" asked Liam, laughing at his brother.

"No! I was too young for the last raiding party. I have no idea what warlocks smell like."

Liam made a grumbling noise. "I wish we knew more about magic. Clodagh says we have lost a lot of valuable information from the old times."

"What are you talking about? Clodagh knows all kinds of spells."

"*Healing* spells," Liam said. "Clodagh's a good healer. But wolves' reliance on oral tradition bit us in the ass during the Great Migration. She says there's a lot we used to be able to do that we can't anymore. We used to work with Fae, and other changeling races like Selkies and mermaids to do bigger magic."

"Do you think some of those Fae races really even existed?" asked Paxton skeptically. "I mean, I know Dad said that elves existed, but some of those sprites and whatever?"

"Yes!" snapped Liam. "This is what I'm talking about. Other people wrote things down and they remember more than we do."

"Didn't help the witches any," said Paxton.

"Yeah, well, fuck the Puritans," said Liam.

Paxton laughed again. "I feel like I'm going to have to start keeping a notebook for you like I did for Dad."

"What?" asked Liam, confused.

"I called them Dad-isms. Maybe I'll create a Twitter thread. Hashtag: Liamisms."

"You are such a dork."

"Hashtag: facts. What were we talking about before?"

"warlocks smell like shitty weed."

"Right. Good to know. And warlocks smelling like shit weed led you to some sort of epiphany?"

"Two of them: one, Mom is paranoid and two, there's a better way."

"Yeah, well your better way hasn't exactly produced a lot of results."

"Yes, it has!" snapped Liam, annoyed. "Everyone conveniently forgets about it because bankrupting warlocks isn't a trophy you can hang on the wall."

"OK, well that's fair," agreed Paxton. "Most of the pack thinks paperwork is unfair fighting. So we don't value it as we should. Sorry."

Liam sighed. He appreciated his brother's acknowledgment, but it would have been nice if any of the rest of his family would recognize his efforts.

"Anyway," continued Paxton, "Mom's been pressuring me to take your place in the meet and greets."

"For fuck's sake!" exclaimed Liam again, throwing up his hands.

"You know what," said Paxton, "I'm going to tell her I'll do it."

"What?" Liam frowned at his brother.

"No, it'll be better. If I'm in charge and I'm here then I take the phone calls and I can call you. And, if there's enough time I can come into town. You can do all the meet and greet formality butt sniffs or whatever and then I can take them back here."

"That is a really good solution," said Liam, impressed with his younger brother. "Let's do that plan."

"Seriously," said Paxton, "are you sure you're feeling OK? I mean, you are agreeing to one of my plans. You do realize that, right?"

"Yes," said Liam. "I also realize that you'll have to come into the city and visit me more. I'm sure Mom will freak out but *I* like the idea."

Paxton chuckled. "I can't say I mind it either."

It wasn't until he was settling down for the night that Liam realized that Paxton's plan also meant that sooner or later he would probably have to tell Paxton about Scarlet. He shifted uncomfortably over the thought until Paxton kicked him. Then he tucked his nose under his tail and tried to let the breathing of the pack soothe him to sleep.

EPISODE 8

THE PROTEST

Scarlet

The Thanksgiving holidays had slowed the protest down. No one wanted to deal with protests when they could be eating turkey. But by Saturday, the security thugs Azure had predicted were out in force. At first, they simply posed with their guns, displaying their threatening qualities like the predators that they were. They expected the protestors to be scared off by the display. They hadn't counted on the protestors containing a high contingent of local townspeople who had no intention of rolling over for interlopers. They also hadn't counted on Azure's well-coordinated professional handling of the activists. Her press releases were pre-scheduled and her troops had go-pros and body cams to record brutality. Something they advertised with stickers that they slapped onto the bulletproof vests of the Blackpool security employees. The stickers were scored like price tags to prevent easy removal, something that Scarlet was sure would be an unpleasant surprise later.

By Sunday morning things had turned ugly. Azure gave the signal and the Lucas siblings sat down. Their wrists were all handcuffed to long chains that wrapped around a trio of trees that had become the icon for the protest—they were each over three-hundred-years-old, survivors of America's birth. The protestors held the line while Azure set the beat, her hand slapping on the pine needle-covered forest floor, and began to chant.

They faced inward toward the trees, their backs to the security forces and the protestors. As Azure's voice rose, Scarlet could feel

Ochre's answering hum like a buzz in her bones. She'd never had the affinity for the witchcraft style of magic that Azure did. The looping patterns and symbology of spells seemed dizzying to her. Azure always said Scarlet wasn't focusing, that she was too much of a daydreamer and that if she applied herself, she could be good at it. But Scarlet wasn't sure she wanted to be good at witchcraft. She didn't mind helping Azure or learning the occasional spell, but she couldn't help feeling that there had to be a better way to use the power she had.

Behind Scarlet, she heard an outcry as the line broke.

"Like the earth," said Azure, although Scarlet had trouble hearing her above the shouts of the protestors. Scarlet felt one of the black-clad Blackpool men kick her back and she jolted forward, bracing herself against the tree.

"Like the stone," said Ochre, plunging his hand into the soil in front of him.

"Like the roots," said Scarlet, her hands were already on the tree bark in front of her, but as the words left her mouth the world slowed and the din muted and slipped away. She could feel the sap pushing up through the tree trunk and out along the spindly branches. She could feel the cold wind in the high tree-top and the pale sunshine on her leaves. She felt the web of the forest. She looked down at Azure and Ochre chanting in unison and realized that they were doing it wrong. The web was larger than the forest. The web went outward. The web contained all. The humans. The animals. The ones that were in between. Azure was trying to close the web and bring up the energy like a wall. That was wrong. It ought to be like really good sex. The energy had to go both ways. Why hadn't she known that before?

Wolf.

She looked down and saw a red thread of energy that wrapped

around her wrist. It pulsed bright and strong and she knew that if she followed it, she would find her wolf. But that didn't do her any good. She didn't need to reach him right now. She needed to reach the others. The ones who couldn't hear the trees.

"Azure."

Azure faltered in her chanting but didn't stop. Scarlet flipped a few branches in annoyance. Azure never listened to her. Fine. She didn't need Azure to listen anyway.

Scarlet reached down to Azure's blue pool of energy and sank another root into Ochre's bright yellow pool. She pulled the energy and then heaved—shoving the energy outward—out to all the little leaves on the web that didn't know they were connected to the tree. For one glorious shining moment, she was everything and everywhere, and then the universe hit her in the face.

Azure

Azure fought claustrophobic panic when she opened her eyes to see two Blackpool security men leaning over her. She needed to get up. She had to protect Scarlet and Ochre. She tried to push her branches upward and then realized that she only had arms and legs and she couldn't remember what to do with those.

"Are you OK?" asked one, sitting her upright. "Did you feel it?" They were kneeling beside her. The trunk of the tree-filled her field of vision in front of her except for two weird black sticks and blobs. The pine needles covered everything and she wanted to dig her hands into them and re-root herself.

"Feel it?" mumbled Azure. Her head was throbbing. Her mouth tasted like dirt. She realized that the two black sticks and blobs were her legs and feet.

"The universe," said the second man, looking around. "The trees. I felt the trees. Did you feel it?"

"I was it," said Azure and both men nodded as if they understood what she meant.

"Do you need help?" asked the first one. "I want to help you." Then he hugged her.

"OK," said Azure, reality snapping back. She patted him gingerly on the back, the handcuff and chain around her wrist clanked as she moved. "That's good. Can you help my brother and sister?"

"I think the nice lady and man are helping them," said the first man.

"The nice lady and man?" Azure tried to focus on making her legs work.

"The blonde lady in the white dress and the guy with long black hair. They said we should help you," he said and looked around. "Oh. They've gone." He looked disappointed. Azure caught the faint whiff of fresh growing plants on the breeze even though it was the dead of winter.

"They were so nice," said the second man, who was still carrying an MP-5 slung around his body. "They said they would take care of your brother and sister."

"Sounds like our parents," said Azure, still trying to focus. The pine needles were amazing—such intricate little spears of brown. Staring at them seemed better than trying to look at anything else.

"Oh, that's so nice that they could be here for you," said the second man and then he hugged her too. She didn't know what to do with that comment. Her parents were *never* here for her. They were most definitely elsewhere. She couldn't imagine that they'd turn up after all these years just for a protest.

"OK, your gun is poking me," she said.

"I'm sorry!" He tore off the gun and threw it on the ground.

"Can we help you get out of the handcuffs? We have bolt cutters. Bobby, where did the bolt cutters go?"

"I don't know!" Bobby was distressed and looked around as if bolt cutters might suddenly materialize.

"I have the key," said Azure, climbing awkwardly to her feet, negotiating the chain the linked her to the tree, and digging in her pocket. She unsnapped her cuffs, but the moment she took a step toward Ochre, the world swayed.

"Careful," said the one who was not Bobby, grabbing her arm and holding her up. His name was probably Kurt or something equally out of an 80s movie. Azure looked around. The protestors and the Blackpool guys were all hugging and milling about, petting the trees and smiling. It was like everyone was on E.

"This wasn't how it was supposed to happen," said Azure, and then felt stupid. When was she going to learn? The second sight was always accurate, it just wasn't always as descriptive as she needed it to be.

Ochre groaned and sat up.

"Yay!" exclaimed Bobby, as if sitting up were a winning goal in the game of life.

"Can you go help Ochre?" Azure handed Bobby the handcuff key and pushed Bobby toward her brother. Her eyes hurt. Every nerve ending felt like it had been exposed to fire. Azure wasn't even sure what Scarlet had done, let alone *how* she had done it.

"Jimmy!" Bobby yelled at someone else. The sound made Azure flinch. "Come help us!"

"OK!" Jimmy yelled back, with an enormous grin on his face.

With Bobby and Jimmy helping Ochre, Azure and Probably Kurt stumbled over to Scarlet.

"Scarlet, baby," said Azure, falling onto her knees next to her sister. She pushed Scarlet's braids aside. For the first time, Azure saw how different Scarlet looked these days. So much more womanly than she remembered. In her head, she knew her sister wasn't six anymore, but it was hard to remember sometimes.

"Scarlet, wake up, please." She patted at her sister's cheeks, but Scarlet's skin felt cool to the touch. Azure found panic clawing at her insides again. She pushed it down and rolled Scarlet over onto her back. Scarlet's eyes fluttered open, but barely and then she passed out again.

"We should take her to the medic," said Probably Kurt. "We have a medic. We can help!"

"OK," said Azure, numbly. She had done this. She had put her family in danger.

Probably Kurt was radioing for the medic as Jimmy and Bobby walked over, half-supporting Ochre.

"These trees are so fantastic," said Bobby, looking up at the foliage. "I can't believe someone would ever want to cut them down. We have to stop that."

"We really do," said Jimmy fervently.

Ochre looked at Azure and Azure found she was having a hard time meeting his eye. Victory had never tasted so ashen.

Scarlet

Scarlet came to face down in a pile of pine needles. Someone was standing over her and then that person walked away. Sometime later, although she couldn't have said how long, she felt hands on her. She was lifted in the air and then everything went black again.

The next time she woke up, Ochre and Azure were arguing. She tried to roll her eyes and then decided her eyeballs hurt too badly. She gave it a moment and decided that sitting up wasn't going to happen on its own. Her stomach muscles protested all the way up, but she managed to get there. Although, she suspected she looked full zombie as she did it.

"No!" snapped Ochre. "No, if you knew there was a risk, you were obligated to share it."

"I wasn't even sure that she'd be here," said Azure. "She is always in flux. She's never focused in the here and now."

"But you knew that if she did there was a risk," said Ochre. "And you said nothing."

"I told you both there was risk involved."

"Yeah, from jack-booted thugs. You didn't say anything about this."

"I didn't know about this!"

They were in Ochre's camp. Nothing appeared to be changed, except the outline of every leaf was like a neon sign. The world pulsed with energy and she could feel the heartbeat of the earth beneath her like an enormous drum. Azure and Ochre sounded like yipping poodles in screeching counterpoint to the music around her.

"Can both of you shut up?" asked Scarlet. "Or argue further away. You're making my head hurt."

"Pretty sure that's probably from working a massive amount of magic that you're not qualified for doing that," said Azure.

"Fuck off," said Scarlet, and Azure looked shocked. Scarlet tried to remember if this was the first time she'd sworn at her sister. It couldn't possibly be. She was pretty sure the lip gloss incident in high school must have involved swearing.

"If you had just listened to me, then maybe—" began Azure again, her tone aiming for lofty know-it-all woman of the world. Azure was five whole years older than Scarlet. That was an eye-blink in the greater scope of life and Scarlet wasn't in the mood to be condescended to by someone who hadn't known how to make hashtags until Scarlet had shown her.

"Seriously," interrupted Scarlet, "Fuck off. You weren't getting the job done."

"You don't know that," protested Azure. "You didn't give it a chance."

"I looked. It wasn't going to work. I tried to talk to you, but as usual, you ignored me. So I fixed it."

"You fixed it!" yelped Azure, outraged. "How dare you! You walked away from everything! You live in a city! You don't know anything about anything! You took a *huge* risk and you have no idea what you're doing."

Scarlet staggered to her feet and channeled her inner stone-cold bastard. She didn't like to think that her inner stone-cold bastard was named Liam, but that didn't make it less true. "I know what works. Your spell wasn't working. As usual, you were too closed off and your ego was getting in the way."

"And your ego wasn't?" demanded Azure. "Did you even stop to think about what could have happened if you'd gotten it wrong?"

"I have to go home now," said Scarlet, ignoring Azure. "Ochre, will you give me a ride to the train station?"

"Sure," said Ochre. He was giving her a strange look, but at least he was quiet.

They were parking the truck in the train station lot before Ochre spoke again. "I'm not looking to start a fight, but Azure is right, that was *really* dangerous."

"Yes," agreed Scarlet. "But you know what they say: be the change you want to see in the world."

"Not funny, Scarlet."

"I'm too tired to be funny, Ochre. I just want to go home."

"Wouldn't you feel better if I took you to Grandma's?" he asked, frowning.

Scarlet hesitated. She might. The open spaces and the empty air would be good for her recovery, but they wouldn't have her wolf.

"No, I really do have to work tomorrow. I need to get home and get some sleep."

"The Blackpool asshats were hugging protestors when we left," said Ochre. "How long do you think that will last?"

"I don't know," said Scarlet. "Long enough, I hope. Humans have an amazing capacity to ignore the truth. Maybe they'll forget, but maybe some will remember. It will help that the entire town felt it. It's easier to hold onto things when more than one person remembers."

"The entire town…" Ochre paused in unbuckling his seatbelt. "Shit, Scarlet. That kind of range… We've never even come close to that. No wonder I feel like I got beat with a stick. How much of our power did you take?"

"All of it," said Scarlet. "So I wouldn't try and work any magic for at least a week if I were you. But I figured, go big or go home." She smiled weakly at her older brother.

"Where the hell did you learn how to do that?" asked Ochre, his forehead wrinkling into a deep furrow. "What have you been doing in the city?"

"Fucking around mostly," said Scarlet. "I don't know. I looked at the web of life and I could see Azure's approach was wrong. She's trying to put up walls. We need to be tearing them down."

"You *looked* at the web of life?" repeated Ochre. "How?"

Scarlet shrugged. "It's everywhere Ochre. How do we *not* look at it? I need to go home now."

"OK," he said. He was still looking at her strangely, but Scarlet didn't have the energy to figure out why. He got her on the train and

Scarlet sank into the seat, pulled up her backpack to use as a pillow, and closed her eyes. She wanted to go home to her wolf. Everything would be better once she got to him.

EPISODE 9

SWOT

Liam

Liam came into work on his own and made sure to email HR that Scarlet had called in sick. He had to hesitate before hitting send and re-read the entire email to make sure he clearly stated that she had called him from her home as any employee might do to alert their boss of an absence. The last thing either of them needed was to make HR suspicious. Then he read it for a third time, trying to decide if sick was the right word, but he didn't know what else to call utter exhaustion. He'd spent most of Sunday feeling unaccountably cheerful and full of energy. He'd returned home and zipped through the round of household chores and errands that had been lingering on the to-do list. But as evening fell, he'd become restless and worried that Scarlet still hadn't called.

He'd picked up his phone and realized that her not calling might have been on purpose. She could have gone straight to her apartment. But by seven he was checking his phone continuously and finally gave in, sending a terse text.

WHERE ARE YOU?

She hadn't responded for a half hour and then the response was equally terse.

AT THE TRAIN STATION. COME GET ME?

It occurred to him as he drove to the train station that he'd never actually called Scarlet before. He'd never needed to. Either they were together or they weren't. The need to call was non-existent. Except… shouldn't he have called her on any of the handful of nights she was at her apartment? At least texted or something. But what was the point of doing those things when their relationship was doomed to begin with?

Liam found her at the train station waiting outside for him and all of his carefully constructed reasons for not being in a relationship slammed full tilt into the reality of seeing Scarlet in trouble. Because there was no doubt that something was wrong. Scarlet was hollow-eyed and covered in dirt. She smelled like she hadn't showered since she left and when he'd leaned in to hug her, she'd shied away, giving only an awkward half-hug. Once in the car, she'd promptly fallen asleep. He'd driven her to his apartment instead of hers and put her to bed. Although, she hadn't let him undress her, choosing instead to crawl into bed in her long-sleeved Henley and underwear. He'd ended up sleeping on the couch because she smelled like too many other humans. There were two particular scents on her—one male, one female—and he tried not to mind that. They were probably her family. He wanted to ask her what the fuck had happened, but he wasn't sure how to broach the topic. He was finding himself hamstrung by all the things they didn't talk about. He had no practice talking to her about things that actually mattered. Well, that and she'd have to be awake to be able to talk to her.

When she'd barely managed to respond to the alarm in the morning, he'd made the executive decision for her to stay in bed. He went to the morning meeting, already deciding that he would go home at lunch to check on her. But the meeting had thrown him another curveball. The Applecourt account was in a full tailspin. Mr. Applecourt was under investigation by the FBI for Russian collusion and possible money laundering. Fosters upper management was in full freak-out. Liam moved from meeting to meeting spouting the same line, spewing the same assurances—Fosters had not been involved in any illegal activity. Finally, Grant, the V.P. of V.P.'s, demanded to see everything on the Applecourt account in person. Liam went back to his desk and realized on the third empty search result that Scarlet had been the one to compile the report.

He went out to her desk and logged on. He had a higher rating than she did so he ought to be able to see the contents of her machine. He skimmed her desktop. As he expected with Scarlet, everything was tidy and organized. He found the Applecourt report easily and emailed it up to Grant. He was about to log off when he spotted a folder labeled SWOT. He frowned.

SWOT analyses, assessing Strengths, Weaknesses, Opportunities, and Threats, were a cornerstone of good business management but they were way above a secretary's pay grade. Internally they could be used by consultants to determine quadrants for improvements that were usually code for lay-offs. Competitors could use them as a playbook to bolster their own strengths and undermine an enemy's weaknesses. He couldn't imagine why Scarlet would have a SWOT file on her desktop. Curiously, he clicked on the folder. There was a file for every team on the floor. He opened Brett's team and blinked in shock. The report was detailed, damning, and utterly accurate. Everyone knew that Brett was a lazy son of a bitch who cut as many corners as possible, but seeing it in black and white made it startlingly obvious. Scarlet's SWOT was exactly the kind of thing that a competitor would love to get their hands on. He opened the other files. They were equally accurate.

He took a cab home. He found Scarlet on the floor of his bedroom rummaging through her backpack. The smell wafting off of the bag was masculine as if it had been shoved in with another man's things. He tried to ignore that to focus on more important details. Her hair was wet and she was wearing a fresh t-shirt. She looked up with a smile that faded as she saw his expression.

"What—" He stopped, trying to find words. "Who... Who are you working for?"

"You?"

"Bullshit. Who are the SWOT reports for?"

"Oh," she said, going pale. He saw the pulse in her neck pick up and he could smell the sweat that was quickly overtaking the scent of his soap on her skin.

"I should have fucking known. I knew you were too smart for this fucking job, and I believed you, damn it. I believed you when you worried about how our being together would affect your job. I fucking believed you."

"I don't love the job. I need the money," said Scarlet. "I can't afford to be unemployed."

"Who are the SWOT reports for?" he yelled.

"No one! They aren't for anyone!"

"So, you just woke up one morning and decided to do detailed competitor analyses? I'm supposed to believe that?"

"No! I..."

"Just tell me if it's internal or external?"

"What?"

"Are you head-hunting for lay-offs or are you working for a competitor? Which is it? Just tell me. Who are the reports for?"

"They're for me."

"Don't fucking lie to me!"

She stood up and for the first time, he saw that she had bruises on both her knees. "They weren't for anyone. It was just for me."

His phone rang and he impatiently yanked it out of his pocket, intending to dismiss the call.

"I can explain this," she said pleadingly.

"Hey Grant," he said picking up the call, putting on his fake calm voice. Scarlet stood impatiently in front of him. "Yeah, I stepped out for a minute. I'll be back as soon as I grab something to eat."

"Arrested?" he repeated Grant's words dumbly, feeling a sense of numb shock. "For SEC violations…"

Still listening to Grant, he grabbed the remote and flipped on the TV. CNN had a live on-scene reporting of Applecourt being escorted into a police station. Scarlet gasped as she read the scroll at the bottom of the screen.

SECURITY & EXCHANGE COMMISSION CHARGES MONEY LAUN-DERING AND WORKING AS AN UNREGISTERED FOREIGN AGENT.

Liam nodded along to the rest of Grant's clipped, staccato speech and knew he wasn't going to be able to listen to Scarlet's explanation.

"I'll be back in twenty minutes. Yeah, see you in a few."

He hung up the phone and put it in his pocket.

"What the hell happened?" demanded Scarlet, pointing at the screen.

He turned the TV off, angry that she would pretend to care about work.

"I have to go," he said, trying to keep the growl out of his voice.

"But…" Scarlet reached out as he turned to go and a discoloration around her wrist caught his eye.

He grabbed her arm and scanned her from head to toe.

"Who were you with?" he hissed.

"What?"

"I know you don't mind it a bit kinky, but it's pretty careless of him to leave handcuff bruises."

"No," she said slowly. "That isn't…"

"You're bag smells like another guy. You won't let me see you naked or touch you. Give me another explanation. Tell me those aren't handcuff marks."

She stared at him, her face a picture of guilt.

"Right," he said. "Don't be here when I get back."

EPISODE 10

RESIGNATION

Scarlet

It took most of the next day for Scarlet to realize that Liam was intentionally avoiding her. Yes, the company was in full duck-and-cover mode and Liam was on the front line, but there was still time between meetings. As the clock ticked toward the end of the day and beyond, Scarlet felt her dream of an easy resolution to their argument dying.

She hadn't decided quite what to tell him, but she thought she could at least tell him that she'd been part of a protest and had been handcuffed to a tree. She'd frozen when he'd asked her about it the first time. It had never occurred to her that anyone could interpret the bruises the way he had. In retrospect, considering the various things that she and Liam had done in and out of the bedroom it actually seemed like a reasonable supposition. But it hadn't occurred to her at all. And now she felt like she was never going to be given a chance to explain that part because he was convinced she'd been lying to him all along. Which, of course, she had been. And if she wanted him back, she was going to have to lie more.

The third time he left the room when she entered, she got the hint and stopped trying. But by the end of the day, she was desperate and decided to take action. Hiding out in Brittney's cubicle, she waited until she heard him come down the hall and open his office door.

Taking a deep breath, she went to his office and stood in the doorway, trying to look confident.

"What about now?"

"What's the point?" he asked pulling on his jacket and refusing to look at her.

"You aren't even going to give me a chance?"

He shouldered past her into the corridor.

"You have some sort of magical explanation?" he said, checking his phone, still not looking her in the eye. "This ought to be good."

The elevator dinged on the silent floor and Scarlet paused to see if someone would be coming their way or going back toward the break room. To her frustration, a man walked directly into the maze of cubicles from the elevators, navigating easily. He was wearing slacks and a button-up under a cowl neck sweater. He had somehow managed the feat of dressing up while still managing to look rumpled. Perhaps it was that his dark, near-black hair—the same shade as Liam's—was sticking up.

"Yo, bro," he said genially. "You ready to go? Don't want to be late for Anna Allanach. Her hotness will only wait so long. Although, for you, she'll probably wait a bit longer. Helllllo." He came to a stop in front of Scarlet. "I'm Paxton. The slob over there is my brother."

"Scarlet," she said, unwillingly shaking his hand.

"Scarlet is just my secretary," said Liam.

Scarlet felt sucker punched. From his dismissive tone to the sneer on his face, Liam had reduced everything they had been to each other down to a tawdry workplace affair.

"I don't think Scarlet is *just* anything," said Paxton looking offended on her behalf.

"Time to go," said Liam, walking toward the elevator.

"Someone's in a mood," said Paxton. "Bye, Scarlet."

Scarlet waved weakly at Paxton and then sat down at her desk and took gulping deep breaths. Her hands were shaking and Scarlet realized that there was no way she could go back to being *just* Liam's secretary. Reluctantly, she opened her computer and typed out a resignation. She included her MBA, apologized for the SWOT, and left anything personal out. This would probably go in her official file and the last thing she needed was to have a whiff of that following her to the next job. If there was a next job.

Scarlet stilled herself and took a deep breath. There would be a job. Azure wasn't right. Scarlet's dreams of a career weren't stupid and she could do this. Obviously, sleeping with her boss had been an error. But she could recover. She would just never sleep with anyone else ever again and that would solve that.

Scarlet put the letter on Liam's desk and took the subway home. There was a problem on the line somewhere and everything smelled like skunk or possibly weed, she couldn't tell which because she didn't do drugs. But her life was misery now, so transportation that took an extra forty-five minutes and smelled like shitty weed was probably her new normal.

She made it all the way home without crying, but the tears came in ugly wracking sobs once the door was shut. She stumbled into the bedroom, gasping for air and unable to draw a full breath. She heard her plants rustle sympathetically as she passed, but she couldn't see them—everything was swimming in tears. She fell onto the bed and curled up into a ball, sobs heaving her rib cage painfully. At some point, she stopped crying, but that only meant that she was laying on a bedspread that was damp with her tears and snot. Eventually, she pulled herself off her bed, swiped at her eyes, and went into the kitchen. She had broccoli in the fridge. Sometimes she hated her mostly vegetarian lifestyle. She opened a bottle of wine and looked for a glass. All two of the wine glasses were in the sink because she'd been trying to pack and get to Liam's before the holiday and had run out of time to wash. There were water glasses somewhere, but she no longer cared about doing proper civilized things. Instead, she drank straight from the bottle, then took it out to the living room and turned on the TV.

"I miss rabbit," she said to Tom Silva on a re-run of *This Old House* as he mitered a corner on some molding. "There I said it. I even miss squirrel. I would fucking kill for some venison." She drank some more and flipped channels then got up and looked in the fridge again. The broccoli hadn't moved. She gave up and went back to the couch, falling face-first into the cushions. Eventually, she turned her head and watched four episodes of Bob Ross while swigging wine periodically from the bottle and trying not to drip it on the couch. Then she burst into tears when Bob Ross said that a happy little wolf pack probably lived right back there in one of his paintings and she had to go find Kleenex.

She came out of the bedroom and saw that all of her plants looked sad for her—their leaves drooping listlessly over the edge of the containers. She patted at one and tried to put on a brave face. She needed to pull herself together. She was going to have to go out and hustle for work tomorrow and she knew she would have to look … not whatever she looked like now. She checked the mirror by the front door. Like shit. She looked like shit.

She went into the bathroom and cleaned the snot off her face, but gave up after that. What was the point? She was going to end up working at some psychic hotline to pay the bills and all of her dreams were dead. She went back to the couch and picked up her bottle of wine. She was going to have to order more wine. Not that she could afford to do that.

She was contemplating whether or not she could blow her tiny cushion of savings on Uber eats and alcohol when there was a knock on the door.

Hesitantly, she opened the door, wishing again that she had a peephole. Liam was standing on the other side, glaring at her. He grabbed her hand and slammed a wadded-up ball of paper into it.

"No," he said, pushing his way into the apartment.

Scarlet unfolded the paper and saw that it was her letter of resignation.

EPISODE 11

SCARLET'S APARTMENT

Liam

"You weren't supposed to see it until tomorrow."

Scarlet's voice was husky, probably from crying. Her eyes were red and puffy. Liam hated that his immediate instinct was to hug her.

"Well, Grant called and I had to go back into the office so I saw it tonight. And tomorrow or tonight, the answer is still no."

He angrily yanked off his jacket and threw it over the back of one of her two chairs. It was the first time he'd been inside her apartment. It was even smaller than his. Although, he liked that she'd somehow covered one entire wall in plants. It made the apartment smell green.

"You can't veto my resignation," she said.

"Just did."

They stared at each other. Liam had spent the entire dinner with Anna and Paxton being furious at himself that all he wanted to do was come back and yell at Scarlet. Anna was hot. She was single. And most importantly, she was a shifter. She had also made it clear on more than one occasion that she was interested. Why couldn't he want her the way he wanted Scarlet? And then he'd returned to the office and found Scarlet's stupid letter. He'd read the damn thing eight times and each time it made both more and less sense. It became more logical to Scarlet and less logical for anyone normal, but all of it, even the parts he didn't want to believe smacked of the truth.

But was it the truth? She was lying to him about something. Was it work? Was it more? Did he believe her letter because he wanted to? The anger he'd been clinging to was slipping away from him the longer he looked at her.

"Shut the door," he growled, trying to stay in command. Scarlet blinked and looked at the door as if she'd just realized she was still holding it open. She swung it shut.

"You're not working for anyone else?" he demanded when the door thunked closed.

She made an agonized wail of anger, stomped her foot, and flailed her arms all at once. It was an entire body refutation and he loved all of it. Humans could lie with their mouths all they wanted, but their bodies betrayed them at every turn. He felt the knot in his stomach loosen. They weren't through the woods yet, but he could see the break in the trees.

"Fine. All right. Where's the other half?"

"What other half?" She really did look as if she'd been crying since leaving work.

"The other half of the bullshit letter. You explained the SWOT, which fine, that's weird that you give yourself homework, but sure. I can see that you're that kind of person."

"What kind of person?" Her eyebrows made sharp angles of worry.

"A nerd. I mean, don't get me wrong, you're hot as hell, and I will spank you with the textbook of your choice, but let's face facts, you're a nerd."

"I don't get to practice the things I did in school and what if I get another job and I can't do all the things I say I can do? I need to practice and I like to excel at my work," said Scarlet. She tried to stand up straight, but that only displayed that one of the buttons on her blouse was undone in the middle. "I don't think that makes me… OK, maybe it does make me a nerd. But I don't own any textbooks."

"We'll buy one. Where's the rest of the story?"

"Maybe I kept one or two for reference."

She wasn't keeping up and somehow that made it worse. She looked exhausted and confused and terribly sad and all of that was like getting hit the gut. All he wanted to do was scoop her up and hug her and promise her that everything would be better. But he had to know.

"What happened last weekend? You said you were going home."

"No, I said I was going to see my family. And I did." Her voice squeaked and her eyes got big.

"God, you are so bad at lying," he blurted out. But that only made him feel better about trusting her. If she was this bad about lying, he would have seen through her the moment she'd actually tried to deceive him.

"It was the truth. I saw my brother and my sister. We just didn't go… home."

"Where did you go?" He couldn't figure out why she was being so hesitant. What was so bad that she couldn't tell him?

"My sister is an environmental activist. We have always supported her," said Scarlet, with a sniff. "She needed help. They were going to cut down old-growth trees. So Ochre and I went to help her."

"You went to a protest?" Liam tried to wade through the gibberish she was spouting. "And your brother's name is Ochre?"

"And my sister's name is Azure," said Scarlet, looking fierce. "Deal with it."

"It's fine," said Liam. "Red was always my favorite primary color. How do you go from protesting to handcuff bruises?"

"We handcuffed ourselves to the trees," said Scarlet, nervously. "The logging company hired Blackpool, the security outfit that beat up all those pipeline protestors. We had to make sure they couldn't move us."

He stared at her in disbelief.

"You spent four days handcuffed to a tree?"

"Only one day really," said Scarlet quietly.

"Did you…" Liam frowned, trying to figure out what to ask first. Attending a protest was so far outside of his realm of experience that he didn't know what to ask.

"Why wouldn't you tell me that?"

Her eyes closed and she made a helpless gesture.

"We don't tell each other things."

That hit him like a sucker punch. It was true, but he didn't want his secrets to mean that she *couldn't* tell him hers.

"And a lot of people don't… approve or whatever. But you know what, fuck it. I'm not sorry. We won. The trees are safe for now."

"You won?" Liam repeated. "I don't understand. Did they… How did you get bruised?"

"Well, we were protesting. If we don't want to look like raving psychos we have to remain non-violent, but it's not like those Blackpool thugs give a shit about how they look and they're probably never going to get arrested and they know it. It doesn't matter. It just… made me really tired. And I wanted to come home. And I'm so tired." Her voice started to shake and her lips twisted unhappily.

She hadn't answered the question, which meant the answer was that some asshole had assaulted his… Scarlet. Someone had pushed Scarlet around and she didn't want to talk about it. Wolves were not serial monogamists. They tended to either be constant daters or with the magical one mate that made the sunrise and set, so Liam didn't have much experience in the field of relationships, but he knew an oncoming meltdown when he saw one.

"And I wanted to get a rabbit before I came home," she continued, trying to blink tears out of her eyes, "but Ochre didn't bring my bow and I got in a fight with Azure and all that's in my fridge is broccoli!" Scarlet ended on a sob and Liam gave up pretending and pulled her into a tight embrace.

"But Scarlet, baby," he said, rocking her, and kissing the top of her head. "You're a vegetarian."

There was a garbled response from his shoulder.

"You don't eat store-bought meat?" he guessed.

The response seemed affirmative.

"I really should have asked about that one sooner. OK," he said, pushing her back so he could look her in the eye, "here's the plan. You ready for the plan?" She nodded. "You're going to change out of your work clothes and into something comfy and I'm going to run out to my car for a minute."

She nodded again.

"Ready?" He gave her a little shove toward the bedroom and then dashed outside. He grabbed up his emergency bag and the cooler from the trunk and was about to head back when he caught the whiff of something skunky. He paused, his nails thickened and he felt his canines lengthen.

There was a laugh from up the street and a door opened with a gust of smoke, light, and pounding bass. The weed smell drifted down to him as two people came out of a house and headed up the street. Liam shook his head at his paranoia and he went back up to Scarlet's apartment.

She was wearing itty-bitty shorts and a tank-top when he got there, which made his tongue want to loll out of his mouth. She looked better. He thought she'd brushed her hair and washed her face while he was gone.

"All right," he said, hoisting the cooler. "Tonight for dinner, you will be having fish."

"Is it sustainably caught?" she asked, but with resignation written in the slump of her shoulders. He probably could have told her she was eating steak straight from the slaughterhouse and she would have taken it.

"Well, somewhat. My brother caught it this morning and that's sustainable right up until he gets pissed off at the fish and throws his pole in the river."

She gave a surprised laugh. "They're so slippery."

"They really are," he agreed. "Go sit down with your bottle of wine and Bob Ross."

"I didn't want to wash my glasses. And he's very soothing."

"I completely understand," he said. He had taken several naps to Mr. Ross's painting tutorials.

She retired to the couch and curled up in a tiny ball and watched him while he cooked the fish and broccoli in her minuscule oven. And then because his nose could only take so much, he opened the skinny kitchen window to hopefully take some of the smell out.

When it was done, he washed her two wine glasses and drank wine while she ate. She looked really happy and he kind of thought that she might have licked the plate if he hadn't been present.

"Do you really like rabbit?" he asked.

She looked guilty. "Yes."

"Why don't you eat meat from stores?"

Scarlet sighed. "I…" He thought for a moment she wasn't going to answer and then she shrugged. "We were poor when we were kids. Our mom was kind of unstable, but she at least was good at foraging. But if we didn't hunt, then we didn't get any meat. So I really don't have a problem with eating meat. But then we moved in with my Grandma and that was a huge step up in terms of stability. Which was great, but after a while I…" She stared at Liam and he sensed that she was saying something that she didn't share very often.

"It's supposed to be a bargain," she said softly, her eyes filling up with tears. "Their life so that I can live. And if I die, then so be it, because I will feed someone else. And if I make it through, then at the end, I'm supposed to go back to the land, to make the bargain complete. Only it doesn't work like that anymore. At least I can pay the farmer for her time and effort. Maybe the industrial farm complex is exploitive and bullshit, but there's some amount of compensation for labor. But I can never repay the cow. There is no bargain with farm animals these days. There is no care. No way to compensate. I can never repay them for what I take. I know that my decision is not for everyone or that it's functional for a society. I'm not mad at people who eat steak, but I just… can't."

Liam felt like he'd been slapped in the ego. He'd been so certain of himself. He had shut Scarlet out and shut her down because he'd been convinced that he knew all there was to know about humans.

"I really should have asked about this before now," he said scrubbing his hand through his hair. "I should have asked about a lot of things."

She was looking at him with those large eyes that looked a little scared like he was going to say something hurtful. It made him ache that she couldn't trust that he wouldn't do that.

"All the meat in my fridge is venison or wild game," he said.

She looked shocked.

"My family does very, very badly with chemicals," he added. Which was the standard explanation and also happened to be true.

"We also hunt all our own meat. I don't like to talk about it because a lot of people disapprove and I thought you were a vegetarian."

"Oh! No. I'm not. I'm sorry. Did you think I was judging you?"

"No? I don't know. Most vegetarians are very judge-y. I assumed you were doing it behind my back."

She laughed. "I really wasn't."

"I usually go back out before Christmas," he said. "I'll get you a rabbit then. If I'd known, I would have gotten you a rabbit over Thanksgiving."

"I don't need a rabbit. But you know how there are some smells and flavors that remind you of childhood? Rabbit is one of those for me."

"I'll get you a rabbit," he said again, feeling smug. It was the first time he'd ever courted a human with wolf presents.

"Thanks," she said, smiling shyly. There was a chittering outside the window and Scarlet frowned and got up to shut the window. "Sometimes," she said, staring out into the street, "I can see the squirrels in the treetops at the park down the street and I think that if I had my bow I could have squirrel for dinner." She blushed and turned to Liam. "That's probably a bad thought."

Possibly it was, but Liam didn't think he'd ever been more attracted to her.

"Yes," he said. "City squirrels are filthy." He didn't add that he knew this from experience, but sometimes they were so fat that it was hard to resist. "Just say no."

She laughed and then yawned.

"Come on, tired girl," he said, standing up and taking the dishes to the sink, "time for bed."

"You don't get to boss me around," she said, sleepily. "We're in *my* apartment."

"Fine, you can boss me around. But we're still on for the

textbook thing, right?" he asked, as she slid her arms around his neck and snuggled against his chest.

"I was thinking a nice thick copy of the Wall Street Journal. I think the textbook I kept is, like, three inches thick. And maybe tomorrow night."

He chuckled. "Might be a good idea," he agreed.

"What time do you have to be back at your place for clothes?" she asked around another yawn as they moved into her bedroom which was mostly taken up by her bed.

"I don't. I grabbed my emergency bag out of the car. It's got everything."

She looked up at him and her expression was very sad. "Did you pack it for her hotness Anna Allanach?"

Liam let out a growl of anger at his brother's flapping tongue. "No," he said firmly. "It's always in my car. That's why it's an emergency bag. It's for emergencies. Anna Allanach is not an emergency. She is a friend of the family. Paxton and I went to dinner with her because she's visiting from out of town."

"Your brother didn't make it sound like that."

"My brother likes to joke," he said sourly, not adding that his mother and Anna had both been pushing the relationship for years. "It's not a thing. Anna is a perfectly nice, attractive girl, who lacks…" He tried to figure out what Anna lacked. But since he hadn't been able to articulate it for the last few years he didn't think he could figure it out now.

"Textbooks?" asked Scarlet and he laughed.

"Yes," he agreed, kissing her.

"OK," she said and turned to the bed, stripping off her tank-top.

"Jesus fucking Christ!"

"Shit," said Scarlet, whirling around.

"That is a fucking boot print!" She opened and shut her mouth. "There is a boot print on your back, Scarlet!"

"Yes," she agreed.

"This is why you wouldn't let me undress you last night, isn't it?"

"Yes," she said.

"No more protests. You are going to *no* more protests."

"I'm going to one next week. They're threatening to remove endangered species protections from eighteen species including the Red Wolf."

"What?"

"There are only twenty breeding pairs left in the wild. We have to speak up."

"I…"

"They're an apex predator. They're a pivotal point in the ecosystem. We need wolves."

"Well, I mean, I'm obviously in favor of wolves. There should be more wolves. But I can't have people kicking you!"

"It's just a sign-waving protest," said Scarlet, taking off her shorts and climbing into bed. "Kicking very rarely happens. You can come if you want."

"I don't…" Liam shook his head. He felt like he'd somehow lost control of the situation. "Maybe."

He crawled into bed with her, spooning around her and trying not to rest his arm on any bruises. His last thought before falling asleep was that Scarlet was not the person he'd assumed her to be, and while he couldn't have been happier about all the ways he'd been wrong, her life was also a lot more dangerous.

EPISODE 12
RUNNING

Scarlet

Scarlet tried to sneak out of bed. She felt like Liam had earned extra bonus points for magically manifesting dinner and figuring out how to recover from being an asshole. She didn't think he should have to wake up at the crack of dawn to go running with her. But she needed the outdoor time. A solid night's sleep with him keeping her warm had done wonders, but she needed to be out under the open sky, even if there was a few inches of snow on the ground and the stink of car exhaust in the air.

She changed into her running clothes in the bathroom and came out to find Liam lacing up his sneakers.

"I was trying to let you sleep."

"How was I supposed to do that without you?" he asked, standing up and kissing the tip of her nose.

Scarlet felt herself blush as her nether regions gave a little throb and flip-flop of desire.

"Besides, I could use the exercise."

"Well, all right," said Scarlet, hesitantly. "I was going to do about five miles, is that OK?"

"Sounds perfect," he agreed.

"OK," she said, grabbing her key and mentally crossing her fingers that he wasn't a plodder.

But she shouldn't have worried. Liam was easy to run with. He had a long, loping stride that kept up with her effortlessly, even when she pushed a little faster to see if he could keep up. It didn't appear to be a problem, so she began to suspect that he could go faster if he wanted. But he wasn't going to. Unlike some men, he didn't feel the need to show off or lead from ten feet in front. Liam liked to stick right by her side. She appreciated the general principle but did miss the opportunity to stare at his ass in his tight workout pants.

By the time they returned to her apartment, Scarlet felt that she had suffered long enough and turned around to kiss him as soon as they were through the door.

"We're going to need to shower," he said between kisses.

"We can do this in the shower," she replied, tugging his shirt upward.

"Good point," he agreed, assisting in the shirt removal process.

They moved in a backward stumble through the apartment to her bathroom, kicking off their shoes and shedding clothes as they went.

Scarlet broke free for a moment to turn on the water, bending over to grab the lever. Liam took the opportunity to run his fingers over her ass and then down and inward, caressing her gently while he planted soft kisses along her spine.

She flung out a hand to brace herself on the wall as he slid his fingers inside her.

"You're so wet," he murmured bending over her. She could feel his hard cock brushing against her leg. "I think you missed me."

"Yes," she gasped, unable to do more than agree. The water thundered into the tub, steam rising and making the wall slippery. She struggled to keep herself balanced as he stroked her pussy. She groaned, more breathless than when she had been running.

"Liam," she moaned.

He reached out his other hand and flipped the water from the faucet to shower, dousing her in a blast of icy water.

"Wolf!" she shrieked and he gave a guttural chuckle.

"That's better." He stepped into the shower, pulling her with him. He kissed her, tongue tasting her lips. His hands, palmed her ass, even as he pressed her against the wall. He pulled his mouth away, kissing her neck. She gave in to her impulses and licked him, running her tongue along his neck, reveling in the salty, sweaty taste of him. She loved the way he smelled. There was something wild about his scent that she couldn't identify but that always reminded her of the deepest woods.

Liam groaned as she licked him again and boosted her up, holding the globe of each ass cheek in his wide palms as his thick cock pushed inside her. She wrapped her legs around him, feeling the glorious strain of his muscles as he thrust into her again and again, pinning her to the tile wall.

The shampoo bottle and then the soap bounced off the shelf as he continued to fuck her, giving her every inch of him in hard strokes that had her moaning and shaking. Her fingernails dug into his shoulders as she tried to keep herself in the right spot. He made her feel so powerful and so weak all at the same time. She could feel her climax building, hovering just out of reach.

"Right there. Oh, God, Wolf, right there!"

She was panting and clinging to him, unable to control her own body as the unbearable tension inside her built.

"Yes! Yes!" Her cries synchronized with his thrusts. "Yes! Yes!" She gave a wordless cry as she came, squeezing her legs around him, her toes curling in tight. He gave three more quick thrusts and finished inside her with a deep groan.

Scarlet buried her face into his neck and tried to catch her breath. After a long moment, she let her legs unlock and her feet dropped to the floor. The water was pummeling the shampoo bottle with an annoying din, but she didn't want to leave his arms to move it. After a minute, Liam kicked it out of the path of the spray.

"Thanks," she said.

She realized then that she probably ought to say something about the lack of a condom. But on the other hand, she didn't want to discuss the fact that her birth control method was a super reliable spell taught to her by her grandmother. She decided not to say anything and hope that he let it go.

He hugged her tighter, snuggling her with a warm murmur that she could feel in his chest rather than hear and she sighed her contentment. It felt so good to be right where she was.

Liam

Liam listened from his office as Scarlet struggled to explain an advanced data search and cross-reference to one of the other secretaries for the fifth time. He couldn't believe he'd ever bought the *I'm just a community college graduate* line for a minute. He shook his head and tried not to smile. This morning's run had been exactly what he needed. Well, that and the glorious fuck in the shower. But running with Scarlet had been wonderful. She hadn't wanted to talk or time herself or do any of the annoying fitness things. She just ran. And that was sooooo wolf. He didn't know why he hadn't been running on his own, but clearly, it was good for him. He'd returned home feeling better about everything. And not at war with himself for once.

Which was probably what had led to unprotected shower sex. He knew he should have addressed that afterward, but she hadn't seemed concerned. And what kind of conversation was that going to be anyway? *Don't worry about getting pregnant, because I can't get any human pregnant. Did I mention I'm not entirely human? Well, haha, surprise!*

His cell phone rang, and Liam flipped it over and saw the unidentified number that meant it was Ferris. As always, he picked it up with a familiar thrill, as if he had just sighted prey on the horizon-line. Ferris was a down-market trader who specialized in buying and re-packaging debt. Liam used Ferris to buy the debt held by very specific individuals.

"Liam Grayson," he said, hitting green.

"Hey, it's Ferris. I've got a fresh batch for you. They hit all the markers and they're all card-carrying members of the Temple of the Unified Vision."

Liam's lip curled in a silent snarl. The Temple of the Unified Vision. It sounded so noble until it was revealed to be a fancy new name for warlocks and the only vision they believed in was one of an earth with humans and no *others*. Death to the shifters and the witches and the Fae. Death to anything that wasn't a boring meat-bag human. They wanted to be the only ones with magic.

It was a constant amazement to Liam that warlocks had managed to decimate the magical population in just a few centuries. In retrospect, the disappearance of the Fae was not a battle lost, but a death blow to every Supernatural species on the planet. No one knew where they had gone, but their absence revealed that they had been the ones to forge connections between the Supernaturals and without them the *others* separated themselves, isolating from humans and each other. And the more they isolated, the worse their problems became. Supernaturals didn't breed as fast as humans and, due to their long lifespans, they always seemed to think that there would be more time.

There was no need to start wars or come out of the shadows, either. There was always another corner of the planet they could go to. Only that wasn't true any longer. Humans were everywhere and with the warlocks pushing them on, they had left their blackened footprint on every corner of the globe. The Supernaturals had been pushed to the rapidly diminishing margins.

Liam's father had often talked about fighting the warlocks on their own ground, as if there was a country where warlocks all lived and they could be fought there. But after Callum's death, Liam had realized that human territory was no longer little plots of land. All humans, including the warlocks, now existed in plastic and electricity, and paper. But that was also their weakness. If Liam could stop them in the virtual world, then stopping them in person was barely even necessary.

"The weird thing is," continued Ferris. "Several of them have recently moved to New York."

"That seems suspicious," said Liam. "I would have thought they'd have gotten the message by now."

"Agreed. But…" Ferris's tone was a vocal shrug. "Anyway, what do you want to do?"

"The same as always," said Liam. "Burn their houses to the ground."

"Metaphorically, of course," said Ferris, who always believed someone was listening.

"Well, yes," said Liam easily because that actually had been what he meant. That didn't mean it was going to stay metaphorical, but at the moment everything he was intending to do was strictly legal. "Send me the reports once you've made the buy."

Perhaps the warlocks in their upper echelons were brilliant masterminds with fat bank accounts, but at the street level, they were the same as any other person in America—swimming in debt. Credit cards, medical debt, school loans, and mortgages, the warlocks weren't any better with money than anyone else. They were just nasty little humans trying to get a leg up by standing on the necks of others. Ferris brought him their debt and Liam drowned them in it.

"I'll have a courier drop off the paperwork," said Ferris who also hated email. Ferris was paranoid, and rightfully so. The warlocks and the SEC were both dangerous to mess with.

"Thanks," said Liam.

"Whatever," said Ferris and hung up without saying goodbye.

Liam looked up as Scarlet walked by his doorway, pen stuck in her hair, iPad in one hand, coffee in the other. She didn't try to be sexy—she just was. He wondered what she would say if he told her that a fascist cult was trying to kill him and everyone like him. She'd probably think he was insane.

His world was never going to sound sane to a normal person. And it was never going to be truly safe for a human. And yet, he still wanted her like he wanted water and air. Being with her was amazing and perfect and made him feel happier than he'd felt in a long time. But being with Scarlet was… wrong. It was wrong for him and it was unfair to her because the relationship was never going to be anything that a normal human had the right to expect. He should never have gone over to her place. He should never have touched her after the first weekend. He should never have touched her to begin with.

Scarlet walked by his office, took a quick glance around, and then pulled her top down, flashing her hot pink bra at him. Then she made a pretend shocked face and blew him a kiss before disappearing again.

Scarlet might be wrong for him, but there wasn't a chance in hell that he was going to break up with her because he couldn't imagine anyone feeling more right.

EPISODE 13

THE DESK

Scarlet

Scarlet hurried from the Evans meeting to get to Liam's office. The meeting had been an absolute snooze fest, which was why Liam had bailed in the first place, leaving her to take notes. Ever since he'd found out about her MBA, he'd gleefully shuffled off all of the tasks he disliked, but were normally out of bounds for a secretary, to her. He kept claiming he was shamelessly using her, except that he was also showing her real-world applications of all the things that had been theoretical in school. She felt like the skills section of her resume had taken a giant leap forward in the few weeks that he'd been "taking advantage of her." He had also said that on the next resume she should put him as a reference and fudge her job title. And that next resume was going to be today.

During the morning break-down, Brett Hubbard had been blabbing on about Kadry Environmental Consultants and how annoying they were and how it was annoying that everyone was using them and how ultra, ultra-annoying it was that they were doing so well that they were going to be hiring. Brett, with his overly gelled hair, perfectly white teeth, and fake tan, had a lot of nerve talking about how annoying anyone else was considering that she was pretty sure his picture was listed in the dictionary next to the word. But if he helped her get a job, even accidentally, she would forgive him. She'd placed a quick phone call over to their HR as her secretarial self and inquired where to send a resume. It was amazing what information could be had by talking secretary to secretary. Now she needed to get her resume in order. There was half a chance she could have a new job by New Years'.

She went into Liam's office and carefully shut the door with a casual nonchalance. Then bounced over to the desk in a way that was anything but casual. He looked up from his computer with a laugh.

"Kadry Environmental is hiring! I'm going to apply. You'll look over my resume, right?"

"Yeah, of course," he said, still looking bemused. "Kadry's what... consulting? Telling other companies how to be more environmentally friendly?"

"Yes! They're perfect for me! I already texted Azure and she gives them a three and a half evergreen's out of five. And I kind of think that in order to get five evergreens from Azure you'd have to grow your own hemp so workers could weave their own clothes, only hire illegal immigrants while paying them a living wage, and power everything off solar, wind, and the farts of cows."

Liam burst out laughing.

"So three and a half is really good is what I'm saying. And the job doesn't go out to the public for another week, and the HR secretary said that if my candidate got her resume in this week she would be considered first!"

"Ah, your *candidate*, right," said Liam, his eyes twinkling.

"Exactly!"

"Well, where's this resume? Let's get going!"

"Printed," she said, whipping it out of her stack of papers and sliding it across the desk.

"OK," he said, yanking a pen out of his desk caddy, and clicking it aggressively. "Are you ready for the red pen of doom?"

"Yes," she said. "As long as I get the job, I don't care how much red ink you bleed on it."

"You say that now, but later, when we're naked, I'm going to be paying for this," he said, looking at the paper.

"We'll see," said Scarlet, perching on the edge of his desk and hitching up her skirt. For every red mark, he made she pulled the hemline up a little further.

He eyed her thighs and deliberately circled a comma. She pulled up her skirt again so that a glimmer of red cotton showed. It was the Christmas season so she had purchased panties with snowflakes that glittered. She felt a little guilty since glitter was a microplastic, but it was the first glitter purchase she'd made in a decade and she thought that the look in Liam's eye made it worth it. He underlined an entire phrase and drew an arrow, so she lifted her skirt high enough that he could see the soft mound between her thighs had a snowflake right where she wanted him to put his lips.

"I'm not sure what that's supposed to incentivize," he said, slapping the pen down as he made it to the end of the document. He reached out and swung her around to his side of the desk. He parted her legs and began to kiss along her thighs, making her shiver.

"It's to make sure you're doing a thorough job," she said breathlessly, as she unbuttoned her blouse.

"Some stuff needs to be re-organized," he said coming up to her breasts. His tongue delved into her demi bra, pulling the nipple above the lacy edge. It peeped there, stiff in anticipation. He sucked at it and tipped the other cup down with his finger so both breasts were free. "You need to play up the diversity angle," he said, coming up to eye-level to kiss her lips, "and your college environmental commitments that you're currently minimizing. But basically, it's a solid resume."

His hands plunged upward along her hips and found the edge of her panties. He pulled her off the desk just enough for him to remove the offending undergarments and then he pushed her back and licked along her thigh, ending with a tongue flick tantalizing at the edge of her pussy. She was never sure what exactly he did down there that was so magical, but she got wet just thinking about the things his mouth could do. He looked up at her, making eye contact as his tongue parted the folds of her labia. Scarlet let out a little involuntary moan and arched back, spreading her legs further and closing her eyes. He had his hands on her hips, controlling her body as his tongue made her roll and shake. She bit her lips, trying to keep herself from moaning as the intense pressure began to build inside her. She let out a shaky breath of air that she hadn't known she was holding and gasped, preparing for the sweetness of her climax, when Liam grabbed her by the hips and hauled her off the desk, and pulled her to the ground.

"Brett!" he hissed, shoving her into the footwell of his desk.

Scarlet crouched by Liam's feet and realized that her ass was still fully uncovered as Liam's door opened. She knew that the wooden apron of the desk was covering her situation, but she also knew that if he got a glimpse at the four inches of air between the floor and desk, he would at least see her feet.

"Hey, Liam!" barked Brett. "You got a sec?"

"Yeah, sure," said Liam, kicking her underwear under the desk and scooping her resume into a drawer in one move.

"What do you think about Grant's moves on the Applecourt thing?" asked Brett, pulling out the guest chair across the desk from Liam and flopping into it. Scarlet used the noise he was making to hurriedly adjust her skirt and shove her breasts back into her bra.

"What do you mean?" asked Liam, scooting all the way into his desk. She was now pressed between his legs. She shifted awkwardly, looking for space, and then gave up and leaned against his thigh.

"Well, I don't know," said Brett, in his peeved voice. He was always peeved about something. "He's being so conservative about everything. I get it, yeah, the FBI is all over everyone. Are they questioning you, by the way?"

"I'm not sure," said Liam, and she could hear the puzzlement in his voice. The Applecourt account was Liam's. It seemed odd that Brett was asking about it.

Scarlet draped her arm over the top of Liam's thigh and ran her fingers up over his hipbone. She loved the sharp V of muscle there when he was naked.

"Yeah, but you gave them all the paperwork and everything, right?" asked Brett.

"I gave them everything the lawyers told me to give them," said Liam. Scarlet, feeling very naughty, let her palm slide down across his front and was rewarded by a definite twitch of his cock.

"That's what I mean about Grant," complained Brett.

Scarlet inched Liam's zipper down a notch by notch trying not to make a sound.

"He rolled over and gave them everything. That's company property," continued Brett, petulantly.

Scarlet ignored him and reached inside Liam's pants to free his dick. It sprang into her hand as she tugged the underwear out of the way. Gently, she leaned forward and licked the shaft. It got harder as she licked again.

"Oh!" said Liam, making an awkward thump on the desk. "Well, you know…" She licked him again and again, and then a little bead of pre-cum formed on the tip. She ran her lips across it, before pressing her tongue to the tip and holding it there. "Sub-poenas," said Liam, as if that were a complete thought. She gently lowered her mouth onto his thick dick.

"Yeah," said Brett, one foot shooting out and kicking the desk, which made Scarlet jump and then freeze with Liam's cock in her mouth. "I guess. It seems like the company's paying for a lot of pricey lawyers who aren't doing anything."

"They're doing what they're supposed to be doing," said Liam.

"Yeah, I guess. But, I mean, you only gave them the official account paperwork and the like, right? They haven't asked for emails or anything?"

"Not that I know of," said Liam. Scarlet sank down further on Liam's dick and then pulled away slowly, sucking gently. His thigh muscles tensed and she thought she almost heard him groan.

"OK, well, I mean, that's at least something," said Brett. "I mean, I hate to feel like we're getting ramrodded. I mean, Jesus, why don't we just suck their dicks while we're at it?"

"Uh…" said Liam.

"Choir boy," said Brett. "It's like you never played sports."

"I never did," said Liam, as Scarlet continued to work his cock.

"Trust me. If you'd heard half the disgusting shit I've heard in a locker room, you'd think I talked like an angel. Anyway, I'll catch you later." Scarlet heard Brett get up, and held still, waiting to see if Liam would try to put her toy away.

"Uh-huh," said Liam, without moving.

"You want me to shut your door for you?"

"Yeah, if you don't mind," said Liam, as Scarlet sucked a little harder. "I was… uh, trying to finish something."

"Yeah, I mean, it would be terrible to have that cute little secretary of yours bother you or something," said Brett.

"See ya, Brett."

"Yeah, yeah," said Brett, and Scarlet heard the door shut.

Liam pushed his rolling chair away from the desk.

"Little Red," he growled. "You should come out now."

Scarlet crawled out from under the desk and tried not to look guilty.

"Turn around, hands on the desk," he ordered.

"Yes, Wolf," she said.

She heard the sound of his belt being unbuckled and then her skirt was roughly yanked up. "You are a very bad girl," he growled into her ear before bringing his belt down in a hard slap on her bare ass. She let out a little yip and he covered her mouth as he spanked her again and then a third time. He paused and she felt his cock tease across her still wet pussy.

"Do you want to be a good girl?" he whispered, his voice a husky growl.

"Yes, Wolf," she moaned, wriggling against him, trying to get him to fuck her. But he kept a hard hand on her hip, and locked her leg in place with his, denying her.

"Say please," he ordered.

"Please," she begged panting, as his cock tipped into her. "Please, Wolf!"

He seized her by both hips and thrust into her so hard that she gasped and jolted forward, her hands skidding on the hard surface of the desk. He thrust again and she bent forward, face nearly to the desk, taking in everything he had to give her. He growled with pleasure and continued to work her in deep relentless thrusts. Her legs began to shake as she neared her climax.

"Wolf!" she gasped, biting her lip, straining against the desire to scream out his name.

He put his hands down on either side of her on the desk and rutted into her hard and fast. She turned her face and put her mouth onto his arm trying to contain the deep guttural groan that came out of her as she climaxed, her entire body seeming to clench and throb. He came inside her a moment later, grinding into her with a satisfied growl.

He pressed against her, flattening her to the desk, nibbling kisses on the back of her neck as she panted and tried to find the strength or the will to move.

"Little Red," he murmured and she could hear the smile in his voice, "you are *so* very mine."

"Yes, Wolf," she agreed.

EPISODE 14

SUPER PACK

Liam

Liam was annoyed. He wanted to be at home fucking Scarlet until she bit him. She wouldn't do it every time. She probably would if he asked for it, but he wanted her to do it spontaneously like she had in the office. It drove him right up to the point of losing all control and he fucking loved that.

But instead, he was with his brother and Albert DeSandre from Oregon. Albert was like three-hundred and some years old and in the last four or five decades had started making the trek out to see their pack every five years or so. He was nice enough, but Liam suspected that Albert thought of anyone under fifty as a puppy.

"This is nice," said Albert, looking around Maxim's. "It was some weird shade of puce during the twenties. I'm glad they've improved matters."

"I'm not even sure what color puce is," said Paxton, "but it sounds terrible."

"It's kind of a brownish-purple color," said Albert, with a shrug. "Is that a human over there?"

"They let humans in if they're with someone," said Liam, glancing over. "That one is with a vampire."

"Oh. I don't know that I ever understood humans, but I feel even more lost of late."

"They're a bit weird," agreed Paxton, picking at his jumbo shrimp. "Hey, speaking of humans," he said looking up at Liam. "I saw yours on the news."

"What?" Liam froze with his drink halfway to his mouth.

"Your secretary human girl. The pretty one. I saw her on the news. She was at a protest."

"Oh," said Liam, finishing his drink. "Yeah, she was protesting the loosening of endangered species restrictions. She's concerned for the Red Wolves."

"Really?" asked Albert. "That's very nice of her. They are so few families left."

"She says there are only about twenty breeding pairs and that they could be decimated in a matter of months if the current administration allows hunting."

"Yes," agreed Albert nodding. "That nice little zoo up in Washington has been doing such hard work to get even as many as twenty. My pack donates every year to their efforts. Your human really cares?"

"Yes, she really does," said Liam. "A surprising amount. I had to listen to an entire soliloquy on why we needed to do outreach to farmers to get them to understand the plight of the wolf and why they should never kill a wolf."

Paxton gave a chortling laugh. "Yes, that would be nice. Too bad it will never happen."

"She's from some rural middle-of-nowhere place called Abingdon. She used to doorbell her neighbors and hand out pamphlets on environmental issues when she was in high school."

Albert let out a dry chuckle. "I'm sure that made her quite popular."

"I get the feeling that Scarlet has always marched to the beat of her own drum," said Liam, drily.

"Well, that gives me hope," said Albert, looking thoughtful. "They all seem to rush about so much and be stuck to their devices. I feel like we've let the humans slide away from us. It's so hard to bridge the gap anymore. That's why I think it's good that you're here in the city, doing what you're doing."

Liam looked at Albert in surprise. Very few wolves understood what they thought of as Liam's bizarre lifestyle choice and to have an elder like Albert approve was shocking.

"If we can find more humans like yours, I think we could build something. We need to be participating more. We all share this world, but we've let the humans fuck it up because we wanted to avoid warlocks and we didn't want to get involved. *Not involved.*" He made a derisive noise. "We're all connected. We can't *not* be involved. Did you see that news story about the protest over the trees? I forget where that was. Somewhere around here. But the town and the protestors came together. They experienced a watershed moment. Those trees made everyone realize that everyone is here *together.* We need more moments like that."

"The protestors got the shit kicked out of them first," said Liam, thinking of the boot print on Scarlet's back.

"Worth it," said Albert dismissively. "And good for them for standing up, well, sitting down, I guess. But you get the point."

Paxton looked from Liam to Albert in confusion. "I didn't see that story."

"It didn't get a lot of press," said Albert. "No one likes it when the rural folk and the peaceniks get along. Division sells more ad space. But my point is: why aren't wolves standing beside them?"

"Too much exposure," said Paxton automatically.

Albert's lip curled. "I know I'm old, and old people always remember everything as being better when they were young, but I swear when I was younger wolves had more balls. Now everyone's all *don't shift anywhere, social media will get you.* Fuck that shit."

Liam laughed, but Paxton looked shocked.

"One time," said Albert, pointing his fork at Liam, "I woke up in the middle of Hyde Park with half a peacock in my mouth that I stole out of a local menagerie and had to sprint across London naked to get back to my hotel. Had to put my fur on halfway back so that I wouldn't scare the shit out of a pack of school girls."

Liam threw his head back in laughter.

"And you think seeing a grown man turn into a wolf was better than seeing a man naked?" asked Paxton, chuckling unwillingly.

"Those were children! And children are blood-thirsty wretches who can get their heads around a few monsters under the bed, but I don't think they need to see my bits first thing Sunday on the way to church. Not to mention the nun they were with."

"That probably would have been educational for her," said Paxton.

"Never make assumptions about nuns, son," said Albert. "Anyway, my point is that I think we need to be building more bridges. In the old times, humans and shifters could mate and we could make werewolves—but that magic is gone."

"I thought that was a myth," said Paxton skeptically.

"Nope," said Albert. "Definitely not. Only no one seems to be doing anything about it. And I don't know what's changed, but I don't like it."

"I wouldn't even know how to begin investigating that," said Liam, frowning.

"Neither would I," said Albert. "But it's my theory that the warlocks and their ilk have managed to separate and segregate us all through some sort of magic. Maybe if we had more cooperation and learned more about the human science and all that DNA stuff we could figure it out."

"I don't know," said Paxton, doubtfully. "Their science seems to be why the planet is such a mess in the first place."

"Is that what you think, Liam?" asked Albert skewering him with a piercing stare.

"A lot of the original damage was from ignorance," said Liam slowly. "And greed. But now, some of them seem to be trying to fix it. The problem is that global transformation is only going to happen if we can shift the burden of change from individuals to corporations and governments." Liam knew he was parroting Scarlet's most recent rant, but it was nice to have a pre-formed speech to fall back on. "The best thing individuals can do is pressure governments to change laws."

"But that's up to the humans," said Paxton, quoting their mother in his turn. "They broke things. It's up to them to fix it."

"Do you leave children to clean up broken glass?" asked Albert. "If they were capable of it, they would have done it. And if they fail then it's our hunting grounds that disappear. It's our water that will be poisoned and dry up. I rather think we're past the point of leaving it to them to clean up their mess."

"What do you want to do?" asked Liam.

"Organize," said Albert. "Our packs have money and resources. I'm forming a super pack." He looked so pleased with himself and his pun that Liam couldn't help but smile.

"Mom's not going to go for that," said Paxton. "Packs are independent. Always have been."

"I think he means a political super PAC," said Liam. "Political Action Committee," he added when his brother's face remained blank. "You want to put the will of the wolves into political play?"

"Yes," said Albert grinning, his incisors long and sharp. "Oh, yes, I do. The fucktards have been mucking it up for too long. Someone should be speaking for the beasts of the field and woods. And I think we're the beasts to do it. We should start putting some of our leverage and funds into action on a national scale. That's why I want to talk to you. You understand the human systems. You've used them to put down warlocks. These last ten years it's been amazing. I think you're personally responsible for breaking up more circles than any wolf in history. And you've barely had to cover up any bodies. I've started implementing a lot of your strategies in Oregon. I've got a couple of pups in law school right now. It's damn hard for them, but they're going to do it. I think we need to move in that direction."

"If you're looking for allies," said Liam slowly, "you won't find one in my mother. Her approval of my lifestyle is tenuous at best."

"I understand," said Albert nodding. "It's like that all over. Your mother's generation doesn't want to change. I feel like my generation had to pick up and move and migrate and fight and we're more used to things going off the rails, but hers had everything handed to them. They expect that everything should keep going that way if they keep doing what they've been doing. Life has never worked that way, but try telling children that. And unfortunately, there's not enough of my generation left. But regardless, you let me worry about your mother. This is me feeling out the lay of the land and getting the ball rolling. You just keep doing what you're doing."

It wasn't until they'd tucked Albert into his hotel that Paxton and Liam had a chance to speak privately.

"The old man is nuts," said Paxton.

"Sounded perfectly sane to me," said Liam.

Paxton let out a rattling snort. "Of course you think he sounds sane. He sounds like you when you're drunk. Only he's serious. A Supernatural super PAC? What would we do with that?"

"We would fund candidates that would do what we want them to do," said Liam.

"That's… fucking vampire shit," said Paxton.

"And notice how the vampires always seem to be doing fine?"

objected Liam. "Mom controls our little neck of the woods, but wouldn't it be better if wolves could travel on greenbelts across this entire country? Wouldn't it be better if we didn't have to worry about oil pipelines across our territories?"

Paxton's head cocked. "Well, yeah, but what can we do about those kinds of things?"

"We can fund candidates who make pipelines illegal! We can fund infrastructure projects that include wildlife conservancy. We could fund scientific research into green energy. We could partner with local tribes to make sure burial grounds are safe. We could do…" Liam saw Paxton's furrowed brow and gave up with a sigh. "We could *be* so much more," he muttered.

"I have a hard time thinking like that," said Paxton. "I want things for our pack, but it's hard for me to apply those same wants to packs beyond ours."

"You're not the only one," said Liam, with another sigh.

"You've always been better at the big picture stuff," said Paxton, frowning. "Is what Albert talking about really possible? Could we make life for wolves better across the entire country?"

"Yeah," said Liam. "Yeah, I think we could. It might even be better for humans too."

Paxton didn't say anything, and Liam tried not to feel defeated as he made his way back to his apartment. He had a pack, but sometimes he felt very much like a lone wolf.

EPISODE 15

DEBT COLLECTION

Scarlet

Scarlet filed the last of the paperwork and turned to Liam's desk. He honestly did not give a shit if she ever tidied his office. He hadn't even when they weren't sleeping together, but she knew the other secretaries gave his desk the once over and then gave her the eye. As if she was personally responsible for his periodic stacks of files. Today he'd dropped off an armful and then dashed out for a meeting that he was already twenty minutes late for.

She sorted through the stack and frowned. The files weren't from Fosters. The files appeared to be background checks and debt records on eight men she'd never heard of. She ran a quick search on the company name at the top of the forms and realized that it was a debt collection company. At the bottom of the stack was a printed receipt. Liam had bought the debt of the eight men in the files. He was now owed a rather enormous amount of money. She took another look at the files. The credit card debt on the greasy-looking Sam Hubbard was so large that it made Scarlet's heart beat faster just looking at it and it wasn't even her debt. Liam could bankrupt every single person on his desk if he wanted. She couldn't imagine why he would want the debt of a bunch of people with icky Nazi-looking tattoos and ties to the Temple of the Unified Vision. Whatever that was. It sounded like a Masonic temple for optometrists, but, if the photos were anything to judge by, these were definitely not optometrists. They look like a bunch of redneck low-lifes Scarlet would have avoided on the street.

As she and Liam had become closer, she had become aware of certain black holes in his life. He didn't like to talk about his family and he didn't talk about the things he sometimes had to do for them. She had thought that it was some sort of strained relationship with his mother and since it wasn't like she could talk about her parents with any openness, she'd let it go. But she had assumed that his work was an open book.

She looked at the files again and felt a tremor of unease. Ever since the misunderstanding about the SWOT reports, Liam had been everything she could have wanted. A drawer had been emptied at his place, there was a space for her toothbrush in the bathroom, they went running in the mornings and he talked about things they were going to do in the New Year. She felt like, if their jobs hadn't been in the way, he would have been open about dating her. But she didn't know what to make of these strange files. Feeling guilty, she hastily put them back as she had found them. Maybe she could ask Liam about them later.

After lunch, the files disappeared and a week later Scarlet still hadn't come up with a way to ask about them. As they approached Liam's pre-Christmas, long-weekend hunting trip with his family, Scarlet decided to let it go. Liam was perfect. The files were weird, but he probably had his reasons. Reasons that were none of her business. Just like Azure's emails with spell-casting and *other*-friendly recipe tips were none of his business. She kept meaning to get Azure to take her off that email list, but sometimes the recipes were really good. Liam had his stuff and she had hers. It made her sad that their things weren't ever going to meet, but she had to keep a level head. Liam was extremely supportive of her—as supportive as a human could be. She was going to have to be OK with that.

Besides the hunting trip was of far more concern. It would be four whole days without Liam and she was already sad about it.

He'd gravely said that he wouldn't even text her because there wasn't any cell service on his family's property, but he'd had the worried look that said he thought she would be mad. She wasn't mad. There wasn't anything he could do about cell service, she was just going to miss him even more because of it.

"Hey Scarlet," called Emma, as Scarlet came out of the copy room. "Is Mr. Grayson still in? His calendar says he's out tomorrow, but I really need the expense reports signed."

Scarlet checked her watch. "He was sticking around for some meeting with Grant and then he said his cousins and brother were picking him up. I don't think they're here yet, so he can't have left. Do you want me to shove those under his nose before he leaves?"

"Yes please!" exclaimed Emma. "That would be a big help."

"No problem. I'll drop them by your desk later."

"Thanks!" chirped Emma, handing over a sheaf of papers.

Scarlet flipped through the reports as she walked into Liam's office.

"Liam, do you have time to—" she began and then looked up and realized that Liam wasn't in the office. Paxton was on his phone by the window and lounging in a chair and against the desk were two rangy-looking young men. They stood up as soon as she came in and Scarlet found herself freezing to the spot, an unreasonable prickle of fear running down her spine.

"Hi," said the first one, stepping too far into her personal space. His breath smelled of whiskey and Scarlet began to curl the pages in her hand into a thick roll.

"You're pretty," said the second one, flanking her like a wolf driving prey.

"Back up," said Scarlet firmly, looking the one in front of her in the eye.

"No, we like you. You'll like us." He reached out and fondled the curl of hair hanging over her shoulder.

"Yes," said the second, his hand sliding around her waist. "Be a nice girl."

Scarlet lashed out, bringing the roll of paper down on his nose and then jabbing out into the throat of the other one. Scarlet raised her hand prepared to go further, but Paxton seized both men by the back of their collars and threw them on the floor.

The office door slammed and Scarlet turned to see Liam. She took a step back, intimidated by the fury on his face.

"What the hell is going on?"

"Our cousins started drinking at ten this morning and forgot where they were," said Paxton, his voice harsh. The two younger men cowered at his feet.

"Get up," snarled Liam. "Get up and apologize."

They stumbled to their feet and stood in front of Scarlet, their heads hanging low, avoiding eye contact.

"We're sorry," muttered the first one, rubbing the red mark on his nose.

"Sorry," whispered the second, and then coughed and rubbed his throat where she'd jabbed him.

Scarlet stared at them. The entire scene was bizarre and now that the threat was past, she felt like maybe she'd overreacted. Except neither Liam nor Paxton looked like they thought her reaction had been inappropriate. Then she felt angry that these two idiots would try something like this at her workplace. She tried to think of something that would make them remember the feeling of shame they were clearly experiencing.

"You are an embarrassment to your family," she said, and they both flinched. "Expense reports," she said, turning to Liam and holding out the roll of papers to him.

He took the papers and she walked out.

When they came out, Paxton took the cousins directly to the elevator, avoiding Scarlet's desk.

"I apologize for my family," said Liam, his jaw clenching. "Are you all right?"

Scarlet glanced at Paxton, who was watching them from the entrance to the cubicles by elevator bay and then at Liam, who was standing a full arms-length away from her. She realized that he hadn't told his family they were dating. That knowledge sat like a rock in her stomach. It was one thing not to tell anyone at work. That was just common sense. And it was one thing not to tell his family's secrets to her. Scarlet could understand that. But if he wouldn't tell them about her then it could only be because he was ashamed of her.

"Yes, I'm fine," she said, smiling politely.

He set the expense reports down on her desk. "I will be back late Monday."

She nodded. He was waiting for her to say more. She couldn't imagine what he thought she was going to say. She wanted to slap him. Or cry. Or kiss him. She honestly wasn't sure which. He wasn't going to tell anyone about them, exactly like she wasn't going to tell anyone about him. Their life together existed in an in-between space that they were never going to talk about. The knowledge of that hit her like a bolt from a crossbow, shattering her heart and her illusions because he wasn't a big city fling. She was in love with Liam Grayson and even if he wanted to keep her on the very edge of his life, she was going to take it because it was better than being without him.

"Your family is waiting," she said. He looked frustrated but didn't make a move toward her. She looked down at the floor, suddenly unwilling to have him see her face.

"I will call you when I get back," he said, trying to catch her eye.

"See you then," she said, smiling at him, although she could tell he knew it was a fake smile.

"Monday." His voice made it a promise.

"Yes, Wolf," she said and saw his shoulders relax a fraction. "Monday."

EPISODE 16

THE HOMESTEAD

Liam

Liam completed his transformation and wandered into his family's house. He grabbed one of the long nightshirts off the hooks by the door, shoved his left foot into one of the assortment of slippers, and then spent an annoying amount of time looking for the match. The original portion of the house had been built in the 1700s, which explained the shitty plumbing and low ceilings, but not why no one could fucking put the shoes back in order. He eventually found the right slipper and shuffled through to the kitchen.

"Hey Uncle," he said scooping a still hot biscuit off the sideboard.

"Hey Liam," said Uncle Marcus with a sleepy smile from his place beside the woodstove. "There's honey in the cupboard."

"Thanks. I think I just want the butter."

"You get anything good?" asked Uncle, shifting in his chair and lacing his fingers over his plump stomach.

"Got a nice buck," said Liam, choosing to omit the brace of rabbits he'd snagged for Scarlet. He'd already gotten a few laughs and odd looks at the dressing house. Rabbit was not his usual game.

"Oh, that's nice," Uncle said around a yawn.

"Anybody out by the fire?" asked Liam.

"Dunno. There was for a bit, but it's been quiet the last hour or so. Someone threw a shoe out the window at the Brown brothers and they finally took the hint."

Liam grunted. His cousins were still in his shit book despite their repeated apologies for the incident with Scarlet.

"I feel like the military has gotten lax," said Liam. "Dad would not have allowed their kind of behavior."

Uncle gave a dry chuckle. "Yes, well your father had extremely high standards and very hard fists."

Liam gave an agreeing noise and finished buttering his biscuits. Then he took the plate out back to the fire pit. He dug a beer out of the cooler, poked the fire back into life, and sat down to enjoy his snack on one of the long low benches covered in cushions. The winter air nipped a bit at his legs, but the fire was warm and wolves never got cold in the human way.

He wished Scarlet was with him. Snuggling up in front of the fire had a definite appeal.

"Hey," said Paxton, coming out of the house wearing sweats.

"Hey," said Liam, smiling. "Were you waiting up for me?"

Paxton looked around and then nodded. "Yeah," he said looking serious. "I thought we should talk."

"What now?" asked Liam, trying to sound amused.

Paxton rummaged for his own beer and settled on the bench closest to Liam, but he looked around again before answering.

"About Scarlet," he said quietly.

"Doofus and Dumbass already apologized like eight times. Although, I'm not sure it counts as an apology if you try to justify yourself by saying how much you'd been drinking and how good the girl smells. Scarlet should have hit them harder."

"Yeah, I figure you already know what she smells like," said Paxton.

Liam frowned, trying to decipher the tone of his brother's voice.

"What's that supposed to mean?"

Paxton looked around again and leaned in. "It means that our cousins may have been drunk and stupid, but I wasn't. The two of you... she smelled of you! The first time I met her I thought it was because you work together, but this time... You were all over her. You're sleeping with her!"

"Ah," said Liam.

"Ah?" repeated Paxton, angrily. "That's all you have to say?"

"What do you want me to say? Yeah, we're sleeping together. So what?"

Paxton looked flabbergasted. "So what? You're going to... I cannot believe this..."

"Believe what?" demanded Liam, angry at his brother's small-minded reaction. "She's hot and extremely compatible with my lifestyle."

"I don't care how compatible she is," hissed Paxton. "We don't violate rule number one!"

"What?" Liam was confused.

"I may have been standing by the elevators, but it's a clear line from where I was standing to her desk and I'm not deaf. She called you wolf!"

"Oh," said Liam, and couldn't stop a small chuckle from escaping.

"You think this is funny? Did you tell her what we are?"

"No," said Liam still laughing. "Calm down. No, I really didn't."

Paxton eased back a fraction, but his posture was still tense and worried.

"Then why did she call you that?" he demanded.

"Because we first got together on Halloween when she happened to be dressed as..." he paused to clear his throat, "Little Red Riding Hood."

Paxton sat back, his normal energy returning. "You lucky fucking bastard."

"And she said if she was Little Red then that made me the Wolf."

"You lucky, lucky bastard. God, you look so smug."

Liam chuckled unrepentantly.

"Seriously? With all the red and white checks?"

"Yes, and stop picturing her naked."

"I'm not. I'm picturing her in braids and that wee little hood. Gah. Seriously, how do you manage to get a girl to do that?"

"Just lucky," said Liam, grinning.

"Wait," said Paxton frowning. "Halloween… That's… She still smelled like you. That's over a month. That's not sleeping together. That's dating."

Liam shifted uncomfortably and dropped eye contact.

"Yeah," he said and shoved a biscuit in his mouth.

Paxton looked around the fire pit area and then back at Liam. "That's why you snagged those rabbits earlier. You're bringing her rabbits, aren't you?"

His mouth full of biscuit, Liam made a half-hearted agreeing noise.

"Human girls don't like that kind of thing," said Paxton, looking shocked.

"She wants them. She wanted to get some over Thanksgiving, but her brother didn't bring her bow. She doesn't support the industrial meat complex."

Paxton looked skeptical. "So you have a protest-sign waving, bow hunting secretary who really cares about the plight of the wolf and doesn't mind dressing up like Little Red Riding Hood?"

"Yeah?"

"I hate you so much."

Liam snorted a laugh in surprise and watched Paxton's nose wrinkle and then twitch as he thought things over. It was hilariously the same facial expression whether Paxton was a wolf or not and Liam tried not to smile.

"But... doesn't it get boring? Being with the same person all the time? I mean, I know when people are mated that it must be different, but I'm not sure... I mean all the time? She's not really the only one you've been with the entire time, is she?"

Liam shifted uncomfortably, then nodded.

"The longest I've been with anyone is like a week," said Paxton. "I mean, there are a few people I'll bop back around too, but you need to space that shit out. But this is nearly two months. Aren't you bored yet?"

Liam shrugged awkwardly. "Scarlet's different," he said, knowing that it sounded incomplete. "I don't know. I'm just not interested in anyone else."

Paxton looked scandalized. "That's weird."

"Shut up."

"I mean, good for you. But that's weird."

"Shut up," said Liam, throwing half a biscuit at his brother. Paxton lunged for it and caught it in his mouth, chewing it thoughtfully, before washing it down with a swallow of beer.

"Mom's going to shit a brick if she finds out. You know she's got you pegged as the heir apparent. Puppies are a must."

Liam sighed and scrubbed a hand through his hair. "It's only been a couple of months. There's no reason to make a thing out of it. I know what I'm supposed to do and I'll do it. But I don't see what the rush is. Mom always acts like I'm going to suddenly go native and start working for an oil company or something."

Paxton let out a sharp, joyless laugh. "No, but she knows that when it comes down to it, she can't control you. And since the two of you rarely see eye to eye on anything, I think she has a hard time predicting you and that freaks her out and makes her try to control you even more."

Liam opened his mouth to snap out a reply and then stopped, processing his brother's words.

"Maybe so," he said at last. "I'm just not sure there's anything I can do about that. I keep trying to reassure her. I keep bringing her warlocks and she doesn't seem to give a shit. We busted up the temple here because of me and at least three other packs say the temples near them have fractured to practically nothing. I don't understand what more she wants."

"Doofus and Dumbass were impressed. They wanted to form a raiding party and go after the new ones," said Paxton and Liam made a half-hearted grunt.

"I'm worried about this batch, to tell the truth," said Liam. "Most of them just moved here. That seems suspicious. I was going to send the rest to the appropriate packs, and then send in debt collectors for the ones that are here. Once we have whatever money they have then we can send out raiding parties if it's necessary. If they're too busy trying to not starve to death or stay out of jail they can't make trouble for us. But if some of them decide to take a shot at us, then we can commit to raiding parties. But even then, I want it quiet. The deaths need to look like accidents."

He got up to throw another log on the fire. He'd probably go home smelling like a campfire, but he didn't think Scarlet would mind. Sometimes he caught her sniffing him. From the expression on her face, she liked what she smelled. It made him laugh to watch her tiny nose try and take everything in.

"Sometimes I forget that you're related to Dad," said Paxton, startling Liam. "And then sometimes I remember."

Liam laughed. "What does that mean?"

"Plan first, act second. Strategy, strategy, strategy. Don't go into a war with just hope and a prayer. Know where the enemy is at all times. Always be upwind of the prey."

Paxton ripped off all their father's favorite maxims in a row and Liam chuckled.

"Is that from the Dadisms notebook?"

"Yeah. Although, those ones are pretty much ingrained in my head. But with you, I don't know... It always seems like you have a plan. I wish I could do that."

"Yeah, I've got planning down, but every time I go to act, Mom blocks me."

"She's worried about you. She thinks you're in danger all by yourself out there in the big city."

"I am. Of course, I could have some of the pack with me, but she won't let anyone go. Theresa and Birdie could be in college next year. They could be with me. I mean, we'd have to invest in property there to make room or accept that, gasp, they might have to live among humans. But I won't be able to do what I'm doing forever. I need more of the pack to step up."

"You think you can do better?"

Liam whirled at the voice behind him and saw his mother on the edge of the circle.

EPISODE 17
Leaving

Liam

Their mother was wearing his father's old black bathrobe. The sight of the threadbare flannel reminded Liam of every family holiday and filled him with an overwhelming sense of sadness. His father had been gone fifteen years and his death was still like a hole in the pack and even more obviously in his mother's heart.

"Do you think you can lead this pack better than I can?" she snarled. Aisling Grayson was tall and her hair was only beginning to take on the gray streaks that mimicked the color of her pelt as a wolf.

"No, Mom," said Liam, trying to maintain his temper and keep his tone even. "I think I could use a little more help. That's all I was saying."

Paxton looked wide-eyed that Liam had even gone that far. Clearly, he hadn't been around the last eight times they had argued.

"A little more help?" Aisling hissed. "You come home reeking of humans, wanting to hunt our food. How are you even a part of this pack? How do you even contribute? And you think you can lead them better than I can?"

Liam took a step back, trying to assess the best way forward. His mother was well beyond her usual grumpy attitude. She was mad. "How do I contribute? Never mind the pile of warlocks I've brought you over the last ten years, how about the fact that I can reset your damn Wi-Fi?"

He tried for a joke. Usually, things got better if he could make her laugh. Paxton choked on a laugh and tried to smother it. But their mother grabbed a small piece of kindling off the stack and sent it spinning at Paxton's head. Paxton snatched it out of the air but looked pissed.

"Mom!" Liam was shocked.

"Now you're telling me how to discipline my pack?" she demanded.

"I'm asking that you not throw things at my brother," said Liam, trying to keep his temper.

"You don't get to use that tone with me!" she barked, snatching up another piece of kindling and throwing it at him. Liam didn't move to block it and it bounced off his chest with a stinging impact.

"Mom," said Liam. "I've had this conversation with you before. I would like you to channel more resources into modernization. I'm not saying anything I haven't said to your face. I'm not using a tone. The only thing I'm doing is telling you things you don't want to hear."

She growled, low and rumbling.

"Right," said Liam. "Right. Because that's your answer to everything—be more wolf. The world isn't built for wolves, Mom, and unless we get out there and make it that way, it never will be. I love being a wolf, but it's never going to be the only answer. We have to be human too."

"Of course you think that. Being a human is the only thing you're good at," snapped Aisling. Liam wanted to be mad about that. It hurt. He could never seem to measure up to whatever yardstick Aisling was using. But at the moment he couldn't seem to work up the energy. He wanted to go home to Scarlet.

"I'm never going to be him, Mom," said Liam.

"What?"

"I'm not Dad. I'm never going to be Dad. Whatever day you're waiting on, where I magically turn into him, it's not coming. One or the other of us is going to have to get over that. I'll see you later."

"Where are you going?" demanded Aisling.

"To bed," said Liam, heading for the house.

"Maybe you should go back to the city!" she yelled after him.

"Maybe I should," yelled Liam and slammed the backdoor.

"She doesn't mean it," said Uncle Marcus softly from the doorway of the kitchen.

"I keep telling myself that," said Liam. "But it's starting to sound like a lie."

He went up to his room, intending to crawl into bed and stay there, but the moon was hanging low on the horizon and sliding through his window and a photo of his family from the last Christmas before his father's death seemed to mock him from the dresser. Angrily, he pulled on some clothes and slammed his gear into his bag. Paxton came out of the kitchen as he came down the stairs.

"You're not leaving, are you?" he demanded.

"Yeah, I am," said Liam. "I'm mad and I'm not getting less mad. Bring me my meat once the dressing house is done with it, will you?"

"I don't think you should go," said Paxton.

"Pax… I don't want to go, but right this minute I don't think I should stay. I'll try it again next weekend or something. Maybe by then one of us will have cooled down. Just do me a favor, and look over those warlock files, will you? And pass them on to whoever is on patrol? As I tried to tell Mom earlier, I think they're trying to re-form the circle up here and that means we should all keep our noses open."

"Yeah, I'll do that," said Paxton looking worried. "I still don't think you should leave."

"Sorry," said Liam, shrugging. "I'll call you tomorrow."

He felt better once he was on the road and decided that he would be even better, or at least happier if he drove straight to Scarlet's. He slowed as he reached the on-ramp. There was a large F-150 behind him, silver-gray and driving in a jerky way that Liam didn't like. At this hour of the night, the driver was probably high or texting.

He swung onto the on-ramp and saw a van parked on the side of the road. It was an off-white, used moving van, with the ghost of an old decal still clearly in evidence. It was oddly perched half in and half out of the lane and while it was hard to smell over the stench of engine and road grime, there was a whiff of something he didn't like in the air. A man got out of the van and waved at him.

Something in the man's face triggered a tickle of memory. Liam found his canines lengthening and he slowed the car further. He was debating his next move when the truck behind him suddenly gunned its engine and slammed into him. The Tesla screeched as he applied the brakes, but the truck behind him didn't stop, shoving the smaller car toward the edge of the on-ramp.

Out the window, he saw the back doors of the van swing open and two men emerged. They loaded up a rocket launcher and he caught the heavy smell of skunk.

Liam unbuckled his seat belt and swung open the door, preparing to jump free. He transformed as he leapt and hoped that he was fast enough.

EPISODE 18
THE WOLF

Scarlet

Scarlet woke up feeling like something was wrong. She paced the tiny space of her apartment and fondled the leaves of her plants. They all seemed OK. She stood still and tried to feel the drumbeat beneath the soil, but everything was too loud and distracting. She needed to get outside and get her feet actually on the ground. She was still off from the protest with the trees. She would rather die than admit it to Azure, but that little stunt had left her unstable even after three weeks. It had also left her prone to zoning out, communicating with trees, and forgetting she had legs. She was getting better, but she knew she had spaced out at least once in front of Liam. Fortunately, he'd just thought it was cute.

The thought of Liam made her sad. She wished desperately that they hadn't left things as they had on Thursday night, but she wasn't sure what else she could have said in front of his family. Friday at work without him had been lame, and now she had to go through an entire weekend before she saw him again. Her plan was to stay in all weekend and stream Hallmark movies while eating homemade kale chips and apples dipped in maple syrup—the vegetarian equivalent of total crap.

Instead, she found herself pulling on her running shoes and heading outside in the half-light of a winter dawn with a nervous feeling in her stomach. She headed down to the park. She didn't actually like the park that much. It reminded her of bears in a zoo—too little space, not enough care. The trees were sad and depressed. But it was the quickest route to any green space, so she took it.

She was halfway around when she got an odd flicker in her peripheral vision, something dark and moving quickly. She turned to face it, but there was nothing there. The air smelled of weed and she wrinkled her nose in disgust. It was a waste of a plant. She knew other people disagreed, but reality was magical enough without altering it with drugs. She didn't know why people bothered. She turned back to the path and went a little further. A man was standing by a bench ahead of her and Scarlet felt a tremor of unease. He lifted up his hands as if declaring a goal and a blackness rose out of the shadows, knocking Scarlet off her feet and onto the frozen grass.

The blackness reared above her buzzing like a thousand swarming bees, Scarlet screamed in terror and brought her arms together, pulling power out of the roots beneath her. The blackness slammed down onto her shield and then reared back, preparing for a second strike. She heard running feet and saw that the man was now running at her with a long knife in one hand. Scarlet sent the nearest tree root upward through the rough, icy dirt and he tripped over it sprawling out across the path. They both scrambled to their feet and as Scarlet prepared to face him, there was the sound of running feet and a fierce and frightening growl. An instant later a wolf seized the man and threw him to the ground, savagely tearing at his neck and throat.

The man slashed at the wolf and Scarlet saw a red line appear on the animal's shoulder. The black form knocked the wolf off his feet. Scarlet mentally reached for more power, hoping she wouldn't damage the trees, and blocked the black thing as it struck at the wolf again. The form wavered and then shredded away like ashes as the man staggered upright and ran away, clutching his dripping neck and shoulder.

The wolf stood up and shook himself all over. He was a tall, long-legged gray wolf, of the kind that had been frightening children in fairy tales for generations. He trotted toward Scarlet and she stood her ground. She did not have Ochre's whistle-while-you-work relationship with wildlife, but she had always gotten along well with most, and this wolf seemed like he was here to help. He rubbed himself against her side, looking up at her with adoring warm, brown eyes. Scarlet took a shaky breath and looked around. No one appeared to have witnessed the attack, but the blood marks on the path were real enough. She looked back at the wolf and he licked her hand.

"Wolf, we need to get out of here before someone sees us. We'll have to go back to my apartment. Are you going to be OK with that?"

He panted in apparent agreement, seeming to smile at her. Scarlet nodded and then tried to jog back the way she had come, but her hip hurt and she slowed to a walk. The wolf kept pace, his head swinging left and right, keeping guard. They made it back to her apartment without meeting anyone and she took the stairs up to her third-floor apartment, hoping that no one would suddenly pop out and comment on her odd companion.

Once they were inside, Scarlet grabbed her first aid kit and brought it to the couch. The wolf was trying to lick his shoulder wound.

"No, sweetie, no," she said trying to get him to stop. "No, I'll do it."

He reluctantly let her push his nose away and sat patiently while she tried to clean the wound. It was only then she realized his fur

A LITTLE RED | 121

was covered in a black haze. She ran her hand over his pelt and came away with a handful of black gunk.

"Ewww," she said and went to the sink. But it wouldn't rinse off her hand, and it was only when she used her powers to force it off that it dissipated and dribbled down the sink. She went back to the wolf and cleaned up his wound, using her hands to collect as much of the black substance as she could. But even after he was bandaged, the black haze still hung in his fur and by then Scarlet felt as if she'd been inhaling car exhaust for three hours. Whatever the black stuff was, it wasn't good.

Once she was done with the wolf, she went into the bedroom and took her clothes off. One hip was bruised and turning purple and her elbow was scuffed. Which wasn't enough damage to justify how shaky and scared she felt. She was staring at the bruise and missed the wolf quietly padding into the bedroom until he had pressed his nose against one of her butt cheeks.

"Eeek! Wolf!" She swatted at his nose, but he jumped just out of reach. He tossed his head back in very evident amusement, his tongue lolling out in laughter. "Very funny! I'm sure you and Liam will get along perfectly."

Thinking of Liam made her reach for her cell phone, but when she dialed him, it went directly to voicemail after one ring. She pulled on her pajamas and went back out to the kitchen for an ice bag for her hip. She opened the kitchen window and tried to breathe in fresh air. The day had turned bright and sunny and this close to the holidays the roads were full of cars and people. Wolf stuck his head out the window too, as if to see what she was looking at.

"You need help," she said to the wolf and he cocked his head, listening attentively. "And I should be able to help you, but I'm all messed up from the thing with Azure. That's my sister. We tried to reconnect a bunch of humans to the web of life. Or I did. I mean we're all connected anyway. I just tried to bring that connection fully back… you know, online. That's not a very good metaphor."

The wolf looked very understanding anyway.

"But basically, I jacked a bunch of my brother and sister's power and used a ton of my own to save a bunch of trees and now I can't help you. And I think if I take you outside, people are going to freak out that I'm walking around with a wolf."

She stared at the wolf who stared back for a moment and then tried to crawl in her lap.

"I think I'm going to have to take you to my Grandma," said Scarlet, hugging him. "I don't know what's wrong with you, but she's been around a lot longer than me and she knows lots more about magic. So she'll be able to help. Hopefully, she'll know what to do about that strange man too. I've never seen anything like that."

The wolf let out an unhappy growl.

"I agree," she said. "I did not like him either. The thing is that I'm pretty sure he was one of the people in Liam's files. I don't even know what to think about that. I wish he would call. I wanted that anyway, but now I extra wish it. I don't think I can wait for Liam. I think you need help and to get out of town. What do you think? Do you want to go to Grandmother's house?" she asked. The wolf didn't reply, but he didn't stop snuggling her either.

The next morning, Scarlet packed her backpack, and after careful consideration, put on her belt and slung on her hunting knife. She and the wolf had slept fitfully, and he had been pacing since the previous night's stealth pee break out in the back parking lot.

"OK," she said, looking around the apartment, "the plan is to run to the car rental place. You stay out of sight while I get the car and then we drive to Grandma's. We can do that, right?"

The wolf looked fully confident. Scarlet wished that she felt the same.

EPISODE 19

OUT THE WINDOW

Paxton

Paxton leaned out the window and inhaled. He felt stupid driving around Brooklyn with his head out the window, but the other option was to put Cousin Conner on a leash and walk around pretending that he was a dog while they tried to pick up Liam's scent. The smoking wreck of Liam's car had been discovered yesterday morning after sunrise and Cousin Deidre in the State Patrol had come pounding on the door shortly thereafter. She couldn't tell them much, but she was certain that she'd picked up Liam's scent trail leaving the scene. warlock scent was all over the accident and Cousin Deidre had banned them all from the scene saying that it would have to be remediated before she thought it was safe for a wolf to get close. Not that anyone cared about the car. Liam was what mattered. Paxton hadn't seen the grim expression on his mother's face since his father's death and he'd hoped to never see it again. Liam had to be OK. He had to be. Otherwise, Paxton wasn't sure their mother would make it.

It had taken Paxton the better part of the day to track Liam across the fields, culverts, and greenbelts with his cousins awkwardly driving behind him in a van. Paxton knew that Aisling, as pack leader, would be able to sense Liam's general movement and direction better than even the best nose, but the pack had been of one mind—Aisling was not to be allowed out with warlocks on the loose. It was too dangerous. So Paxton was the one who had gone, and Aisling had not been happy about it. But sometimes the pack leader got outvoted.

Liam's trajectory had become quickly obvious, but what no one could figure out was why Liam had gone to the city instead of coming home. And the gods only knew how no one had noticed him crossing the Brooklyn Bridge. Or maybe they had. Paxton had already spotted someone jogging in the snow in nothing but gold lame bike shorts and earmuffs. Maybe in the city, a wolf crossing the Brooklyn Bridge was the least weird thing someone was going to see at four in the morning.

"Right," barked Paxton, catching a niggling little hit of Liam.

Conner swerved right at the next corner.

He inhaled again, picking up the woodsy floral scent of spring wrapped up in human femaleness, and realized exactly where his brother had gone. But directly behind the smell of Scarlet was the skunky dark smell that made him want to sneeze.

"warlocks, too," said Paxton, looking into the back of the van. "Get ready." The Brown brothers looked at each other and held out their hands for rock-paper-scissors—Devin lost and reached for his gun. Derek pulled off his shirt. Paxton, already half-naked, stripped out of his pants.

The sun was barely beginning to crack the heavy, flat clouds full of snow above them when Paxton spotted Liam. He was in wolf form on the corner of a vacant and overgrown lot. He was standing back-to-back with Scarlet who had a long hunting knife in one hand. They were facing four warlocks, and as he watched, a black cloud formed and struck at Scarlet. She dodged right and lunged at the nearest warlock, slicing through the black cloud and into his arm and chest. When the warlock tried to avoid her, Liam lunged and tackled him, pulling him to the ground. The man gave a guttural yell, but the other two warlocks stepped forward and the black cloud doubled in size, sweeping down and slamming into Scarlet, flinging her off her feet. She tumbled into the overgrown debris and snow-covered grass of the lot, sprawling awkwardly. One of the warlocks charged at her, pulling a knife that was close to a foot long and had a black blade.

Paxton's heart was in his throat, his claws already shredding through his fingertips as Scarlet rolled, narrowly avoiding the warlock's downward slice. She stabbed upward, making contact, but as she shoved her knife into his shoulder the black cloud struck at her again, hammering her to the ground. Liam dropped the warlock he had hold of and sprinted toward Scarlet, just as Conner pulled the van to a screeching halt.

Paxton heard the back doors slam open behind him, but he was already out of the van and running toward his brother. He didn't remember changing, he only remembered the burning cold of snow under his paws. He heard the hot pop, pop of Devin's gun, but he already had his jaws around someone's throat. He squeezed tight and then ripped, twisting his head sharply. He felt flesh tear and the sudden gush of blood. The body under him went limp and Paxton gave it an extra shake, for certainty, and then let go and looked around.

He shifted and looked around again through human eyes. Liam was standing over Scarlet's unconscious body, watching them warily. The other warlocks were dead. Paxton couldn't tell who was responsible for what damage. He supposed it didn't matter, but his stomach was roiling and he wanted to lick the snow to get the taste of warlock out of his mouth. He tried to pull himself together. He didn't want the Brown brothers to think he was an idiot. They already looked down on any of the pack who hadn't gone into the military.

"Liam," said Paxton. "Change back. We've got to go."

Liam continued to watch him with the same distrustful expression. In the distance, they heard sirens.

"We've got to go," said Devin.

"Liam!" barked Paxton. "Let's go. Come on. Change!"

Liam jumped a little at Paxton's tone but didn't move.

"I don't think he can," said Conner. "Look at him. He's not…" Conner trailed off and they all stared at Liam. Paxton felt a hit of adrenalin and panic as he realized what Conner meant. The wolf in front of him was definitely Liam, he was also definitely all wolf. There wasn't anything human in the way he was watching them. It wasn't unusual for pups to get stressed and stuck in one shape or another, but this didn't feel the same.

"Liam," said Paxton, taking a step forward. Liam's jowls lifted in a silent snarl and Paxton stopped. He was both freezing and sweating at the same time. It was as though Liam wasn't Liam anymore. What was he supposed to do?

"Derek," Paxton said, turning to his still wolf-shaped cousin. "Talk to him."

Derek took a cautious pace forward. Liam in wolf form or out was bigger and outweighed him. Derek didn't want to piss Liam off. There was the subtle tail flip and head cock as Derek tried to communicate. *The pack has to go. Danger approaches.*

Liam shifted, clearly undecided. He wanted to go, but something was holding him back. Paxton tried to think of the right thing to do. He felt stupid. Liam was always the one with a plan, the one who knew what to do.

"Tell him we'll bring Scarlet," said Paxton.

Derek nodded which was odd in wolf form and gave everyone the brain twist of communicating in multiple languages and multiple shapes. Then he turned back to Liam. Paxton watched carefully and then moved closer and reached for Scarlet. Liam whined but moved away from her, letting Paxton haul her up off the ground and over his shoulder.

"Devin, grab her knife out of that warlock. Sweep the area and then let's go."

"On it," said Devin, nodding and already moving to follow orders. Paxton felt a tiny loosening of his shoulder muscles to know that the pack was following his orders, but it wasn't until they were all in the van and driving at a cautious and law-abiding speed away from the scene that he breathed a sigh of relief.

"Put your pants on," said Conner, his eyes glued to the road.

"What?" asked Paxton, startled.

"Nothing says guilty like driving around naked."

Paxton looked down at himself. "Right," he said, reaching down onto the floor for his clothes. He had just pulled on his shirt when a cop car zoomed by, heading toward the area where they'd left the warlock bodies. Paxton acted casual until they were in the rear-view mirror and then pulled on his pants, bridging in the seat to pull them on. When he was done, Devin handed him his socks and boots from the backseat.

"How's he doing?" asked Paxton, taking his footgear, and looking back to where Liam was laying down next to the still unconscious Scarlet.

"I don't know," said Devin.

"I'm not sure about her either," said Derek. "I think we need to get them both back to Clodagh."

Paxton nodded. He hoped the pack's healer would know what to do because Paxton sure as hell didn't.

"We're in such deep shit," muttered Conner, hunching over the steering wheel.

"Yeah," said Paxton. "I know."

EPISODE 20

THE HOMESTEAD

Scarlet

Scarlet regained consciousness in jolting waves of memory and sensations. They had been chased and she had run to the nearest wild place she could find, but the vacant lot hadn't contained much she could use. They had fought. Some other men had pulled up in a van? She wasn't sure. She remembered cutting into one of their attackers, but nothing after that.

She sat up with a groan. Her head ached and the bruise from the previous day throbbed. She was in a bedroom. On a bed. With a worn green quilt. She swung her feet over the edge and tried to stand, but then seized the tall, carved bedpost as her knees failed to hold her. She stayed there for a long moment and only when she could stand reliably did she move her hand to see what kind of sharp and pointy carving she was grabbing. It was a wolf's head, his mouth open, frozen mid-snarl.

"Well, that's a pleasant thing to sleep with," she muttered.

She staggered to the window and looked out. It was a pastoral scene. Eighteenth-century outbuildings, a wide lawn covered in snow, and nothing but trees in the distance. She turned back to the room. The furniture was all antique and made of oak, marked with a heavy patina. She saw herself in the wavering mirror over the dresser and winced. She had blood smeared on one side of her face and mud on the other. She tried to wipe it off and smooth down her hair, then she went to the door, determined to find out where she was.

The door was locked.

Scarlet stepped back and considered her options. She wasn't particularly sure of her magic right at the moment, and iron was always hard to work with. She was about to try the window when she heard the sound of the key being turned in the lock.

A woman entered, carrying Scarlet's backpack. She was tall with only a few silver strands threaded through her dark hair and she was wearing a long, loose gray dress.

"We have sent for a car," she said, dropping the pack on the bed as if it were disgusting. "You will return to your home when it arrives."

Scarlet scratched her head, puzzled.

"All right. But who are you?"

"That doesn't matter," the woman said firmly. "You will leave and you will forget you were ever here."

"That seems unlikely," said Scarlet. "Where is my wolf?"

The woman took an aggressive step forward, her hands clenching in fists at her sides, but she stopped, seeming to vibrate in anger.

"He is *not* yours!"

"Yes, he is. And I want him back."

"He was *never* yours. There is no back. There is no future. You will leave and you will never come back."

"I want my wolf," said Scarlet.

The woman made a snarling, angry noise and turned on her heel. Scarlet realized, too late, that the woman was going to lock her in again and ran after her, reaching the door as it shut.

"Bring me my wolf!" she screamed out the words in fury and slapped the door, her power adding an ominous boom to the sound that probably echoed across the entire building. Almost immediately a lonesome wolf began to howl in a long wavering note.

Scarlet wanted to cry. She didn't know what was going on. Her head felt jumbled, like she'd been tossed around in a drier for a week, but she knew with certainty that the woman was wrong. That was *her* wolf. And right now he was someplace without her.

Sniffing fiercely, Scarlet straightened up and put her shoulders back. She'd tried childish and demanding and gotten nowhere. It was time to be smarter. She took a deep breath, trying to center herself, and was surprised to find it was easy. There was none of the everyday clutter of life here. A low buzz of electricity was the only background interference. She could feel the deep exhalation of the forest outside the window. The place, despite the angry woman locking her in a bedroom, was a good place.

Scarlet pulled on her backpack and went to the window. It was sealed shut, of course. She prepared herself and then grabbed the spindly little chair by the bed and threw it through the window.

Moments later the door flew open and a man ran in.

"She's climbed out the window!" He yelled, running past her and staring at her illusion as it climbed down the rocky face of the house. He ran out of the room and Scarlet followed him, clinging carefully to the illusion that she was *not here*. The man roused the household and there was a great commotion as several people went immediately to chase her. But downstairs, Scarlet heard the angry snarl of a wolf who wasn't going anywhere.

Scarlet followed the noises, creeping along a dark passageway with a low ceiling. She heard another angry growl and she hurried forward to a door, swinging it open all in a rush. The wolf was in a cage.

"What did they do?" she gasped, hurrying forward and dropping to her knees outside the cage. "Oh, if they have hurt you I will murder them." The wolf came promptly to the cage door and tried to lick her through the bars as she struggled with the lock. It was only looped through the clamp to keep the door shut, but it was heavy and awkward and her fingers were stiff and cold.

"Scarlet, stop."

Scarlet whirled, the lock-in her hand, the door swinging open.

"Paxton?" Scarlet stared at Liam's brother in confusion.

"Scarlet, he's not safe. You have to leave him in there."

"No," said Scarlet, "he's fine." As if to prove her point the wolf licked the entire side of her face. "That's not helping, sweetie. Paxton, I don't understand. Where am I? Where's Liam?"

Paxton looked at the wolf and his expression was an agony of grief and suddenly Scarlet realized how stupid she had been. She looked at the wolf who was truly her Wolf.

"No..."

But his eyes were the same brown as Liam's and his hair was the same black.

"Make him change back," she whispered, still staring at Liam.

"We can't," said Paxton, his voice anguished. "We've tried everything. Whatever the warlocks did, we can't undo it. We've put in a call to Seattle. They have a shaman who might be able to help. We're not giving up hope."

She looked up into Paxton's face and saw that while hope might not be dead, it was only a flickering candle in a storm and one tiny gust would put it out.

"I can help," she said. "I mean, not right this second exactly, but..."

"Paxton!" The door into the hall was suddenly filled by the woman from upstairs and if she had been angry before, she was furious now. "Get her out of here!"

"Mom," said Paxton, "just stop for a minute."

"I will not stop," hissed the woman. "She doesn't belong here, let alone within ten feet of him!"

Scarlet felt like she'd been slapped. Everything hurt, her boyfriend had been lying to her and now his mother hated her. Scarlet crawled into the cage with the wolf and shut the door behind them.

"What are you doing?" his mother demanded. "Get out of there."

"No," said Scarlet and turned her back on them.

"Stop being a child. Come out of there at once!"

Scarlet didn't bother to reply. Instead, she put her arms around Liam's neck and buried her face in his fur. He made the warm rumbly sound he always made when she hugged him and Scarlet let out a little sob.

"I am—"

Whatever the woman had been going to say was cut off as Paxton pushed her out onto the hall and slammed the door shut.

When they didn't return after a few minutes, Scarlet took off her backpack and lay down in the cage. The wolf promptly lay down with her, snuggling into a good spooning position.

"Your mom isn't going to believe me, is she? That I can help and that we should take you to my grandma, I mean."

He gave a deep sigh and looked at her out of the corner of his eye.

"And if Grandma can't help, and you don't turn back, your mom will never let us stay together."

The wolf didn't respond.

"It's fine," said Scarlet. "We'll go tonight. It will probably mean that I'll have to figure out *traveling*, which admittedly I've never done, but I was going to have to figure it out sooner or later. And then if Grandma can't help us, then we'll just… go to… Canada. There are some nice deep woods in Canada and I don't need a job anyway. Our ancestors didn't need jobs. I'm sure we'll be perfectly happy there."

The wolf picked up his head and gave her a very Liam-ish look.

"Don't give me that look. It's a backup plan. I'm sure Grandma can fix you. I'm sure of it. We'll go tonight after everyone is asleep."

The wolf licked her face and lay back down again. Scarlet hugged him tight to her and tried to remember everything her Grandma had ever said about *traveling*.

EPISODE 21

searching

Paxton

Paxton stood in the doorway and watched as his mother ordered the loading of the vans. She was going to go to the city and get her son back from *that human harlot.*

They had woken this morning to an empty cage. His mother had blamed him because he was the one who had convinced her to let Scarlet stay. He was still convinced that had been the right decision. Liam had been more human with Scarlet. And Scarlet had said she could help. He wasn't sure how, but for a human she had seemed very unbothered by Liam's wolf status or the warlocks.

Great Aunt Bryn sidled up to him.

"I think your mum's got the wrong end of the stick on this one."

"She says she knows where he's going," said Paxton doubtfully. "The alpha awareness…"

Aunt Bryn looked around carefully.

"It just says he's in the woods," she whispered, leaning in close.

"Which woods?" Paxton whispered back, gesturing at the panoply of trees that surrounded the house.

Aunt Bryn shook her head. "She doesn't know."

Paxton rolled his head around on his neck nervously. Saying an alpha didn't know something that they claimed to know was asking to get into a fight.

"So, somehow Scarlet has done something to the alpha awareness?" suggested Paxton. Aunt Bryn shrugged her confusion.

Paxton mulled it over. His mother had been annoyed last night, but now she was in a full-on rage, which probably meant that she had come to the same conclusion.

"The alpha awareness isn't the only way to find someone," murmured Aunt Bryn.

"I took a sniff around myself. The tracks end at the woods."

"Last night when you was arguing with Aisling, I heard the girl talking to Liam," said Bryn. "She said she wanted to take him to her Grandma and that her Grandma could help."

"Her Grandma…"

"They say that there are actual witches in some places still," continued Bryn. "And you can't tell me that a human could sneak past twenty wolves and the patrol guards, even with Liam helping."

"That's what I'm saying! Something isn't normal with her! She smells human, but there's something else going on. And if she's messed with the alpha awareness then that just proves my point. Only Mom won't listen."

"Nah, she won't," agreed Bryn. "And do we really think that because those footprints they found are going toward the city that's really where they're going?"

"No," said Paxton, remembering one of the few facts he knew about Scarlet. "We think she's going to her grandmother in Abingdon. And that's where I'm going. Cover for me with Mom."

Aunt Bryn nodded. "Good luck," she whispered as he turned back into the house and ran for the back door.

Scarlet

Scarlet leaned against a birch tree, panting. The wolf pressed against her side and growled at the shuddering, swaying shadows of the woods that were not woods. In one hand she held the thin green line that connected her to her grandmother. Her other hand was tangled in a red line that also wrapped around Wolf.

"We're almost there," she said. "Just a little further."

All forests were connected. With a little bit of focus and power, it was possible to *travel* across the in-between places and come out in another wood. Scarlet knew that her grandmother could do it easily and that Azure had done it at least twice, so obviously Scarlet should be able to do it too. It was just that right now she was finding it harder than she had anticipated.

She looked at Wolf, vibrant neon rainbows flexed in and out of his shape and she blinked trying to clear the afterglow. She'd heard other people describe being on drugs—this seemed like a similar experience. Nervously, she clutched at the tenuous threads that anchored her to her family and the wolf. If she didn't get this right, they would be lost in the fairy woods forever.

"OK," she said, gathering her strength and taking a firmer grip on the green thread. "One last push." She smiled reassuringly at Wolf, who looked worried. "We got this."

Holding tight to the green and red threads she stumbled forward, leaning against a force that couldn't be seen. The wolf stayed at her side, giving her his strength. She pushed through whipping branches and underbrush and then the force abruptly gave way and she fell face-first into a cold, wet pile of snow.

Slowly she picked herself up and looked around. Her grandmother's farm was ahead of them. Dawn was a wan, pale thing that was creeping above the tree-line as if trying not to be noticed. Scarlet wanted to be happy that she'd arrived, but she felt exhausted and on the point of tears.

"Come on, Wolf," she said, climbing wearily to her feet. They stumbled down the muddy drive and Scarlet wrapped her arms around herself, shivering. The farmhouse door opened and a warm, yellow shaft of light spilled out. She could see her grandmother's silhouette in the doorway and she hurried forward eagerly, flinging herself into her grandmother's arms and breathing out a shaky sob of relief.

"It's all right," said Diana Lucas, holding her tight. "You're home now."

"Oh, Grandma," said Scarlet with a sniffle. "We're in such trouble."

"Well, I can see the trouble," said Diana, leaning back and swiping a finger across the mud on Scarlet's face. "But who is the *we*? Who is this you have with you?"

Scarlet stepped back and stood beside Wolf. "Um, Grandma this is my boyfriend, Liam."

"I see."

"But he's stuck in this shape. I think it's warlock magic. They attacked us."

"Ah," said Diana. "Nasty creatures."

"He's covered in this black gunk. I tried to get it off of him, but I'm still sort of…"

"Unstable because of that little stunt you pulled with Azure and Ochre?" Scarlet nodded and her grandmother's face said *I told you so* as surely as any words. "So, of course, you thought *if I can't do that then I should definitely try traveling?*"

"I had to get us here. His family wouldn't listen to me. And it's magic I understand. I don't know about warlock magic."

Diana shook her head again. "Well, stop standing on the porch like a stranger and go on into the kitchen. We'd best get it sorted out."

Scarlet led the wolf into the kitchen and then stood dripping in the middle of the tile floor.

"Off with the clothes," yelled her grandmother from the laundry room. "You're making puddles."

Slowly, Scarlet stripped down to her underwear and bra.

"Well, my," said her grandmother coming out with a basketful of supplies under one arm and a nightgown in the other hand. "Aren't you fancy?"

"It's the Christmas season," said Scarlet, attempting to be dignified.

"In your pants apparently," said Diana, her eyes twinkling. "Take your things into the laundry room and wash up. I'll warm up your nightgown on the stove."

"Thanks," muttered Scarlet, taking her wet things into the wash sink. She scrubbed up and came back pink-cheeked and shivering. Diana pulled the nightgown off the pot-bellied wood stove and handed it over. Scarlet pulled on the long, old-fashioned nightgown and turned to see what her grandmother was doing to Liam. He was now sitting in a circle of salt and looking most put upon.

"You pop in there with him," said Diana. "Give him a bit of a rub down with this." She handed over a dish full of lavender-smelling oil and an evergreen sprig. "He'll probably hate the smell, but it'll do the trick while I smudge him up. The warlock's magic is usually bacterially based. It can change body chemistry. It'll take him a while to clear up once we're done, but he should be OK."

"Bacteria," repeated Scarlet wrinkling her nose. "So, they're like the chemical warfare of magic?"

Her grandmother let out a surprised laugh. "Yes. I hadn't thought of it like that, but yes, I suppose so. Their goal is usually to cleanse the earth of the demon races and of course keep women in their God-ordained role of servitude. Blah, blah, blah, men are great, look at our penises, the usual. They founded the Spanish

Inquisition and sided with the Nazis, so you can imagine what kind of people they are."

"Witch killers," said Scarlet, frowning in disapproval. "Why didn't you tell me about them?"

"I've told you about the inquisitions and the evil forces. They have called themselves different things over time. And there haven't been that many around here for the last ten or fifteen years or so. The local Temple had some financial trouble and sort of flamed out. And just when I might have started telling you how to deal with that kind of magic, you went off to college. So, there's that."

Scarlet splashed oil on Liam rather more vigorously than necessary and he gave her side-eye, which from a wolf was quite strong.

"Ochre went to college," Scarlet muttered.

"Ochre's major aligns more closely with magic and he's just…"

"Just what?" demanded Scarlet.

"More traditional."

"What's so great about being traditional? Traditional got us right where we are and it's not going to get us out. We have to think new thoughts and do new things."

"Possibly, but we don't have to do dangerous new things that could get us killed."

Scarlet hesitated. "I'm not trying to get anyone killed."

"You're going to get *you* killed if you're not more careful," said Diana.

"I am careful!"

"How? When?"

"Generally, I'm very careful," protested Scarlet.

"Really?" Diana gestured to Liam. "This doesn't look careful. That protest wasn't careful."

"Azure's spell wasn't going to accomplish anything," said Scarlet. "I would have talked to her about it, but she ignores me. And as a result, the last I heard, several Blackpool employees have moved to that town and filed complaints against Blackpool and the logging company. The town has filed an injunction to protect the trees. People are coming together. What I did worked."

"You risked your life and Azure and Ochre's lives. You should have been more careful. And obviously, you're not being any more careful in the city."

"I will admit that I could have... tried harder to talk to Azure at the protest," said Scarlet. "But I'm not unsafe in the city. Things are usually fine. I don't know how I'm responsible for warlocks attacking my boyfriend."

Diana sighed. "I'm not saying you are. I'm saying the city itself is unsafe."

"Meh," said Scarlet. "Bad things happen everywhere. I have a vision, Grandma. I don't mean like a second sight thing like Azure. But a goal. I think the world can be changed. I think we can fix things. I think humans can care like we care. I think they can reconnect to the Earth. The results of the protest are proof that I'm right. And I want to do more of that. But I can't do it from here on the farm. I need to be out there with humans."

"And your wolf boyfriend?" asked Diana drily, as she laid out her tools on a piece of beige felt.

"Well, OK, so I did not realize he was a wolf at the time we met," said Scarlet. "But I'm not speciesist, so it doesn't matter to me."

"Mm-hmm," said Diana. "You may find that it matters to the wolves."

"I think his mom hates me," said Scarlet, suddenly feeling depressed. "She said she didn't want me around Liam."

"Mmm," said Diana.

"He was going to bring me home rabbits," said Scarlet sadly.

"And we were going to watch the ball drop from Maxim's on New Year's."

"Well, I'm sure you can still do that," said Diana. "Now hush while I concentrate."

Diana lit a sage bundle and the smoke wavered up from the dry sticks and curled around Liam, clinging to the fur, particularly everywhere that Scarlet had rubbed the oil. She rubbed on more oil and tried not to worry that her Grandmother couldn't fix him. She didn't really want to move to Canada.

When Liam was wreathed in smoke, Diana gestured for Scarlet to step out of the ring of salt. When Scarlet was safely on the other side, Diana reached out and touched Liam's forehead. Scarlet felt a deep sort of bounce like a spring coming back to its original position after being stretched out and the oil flew off his fur and lodged in the salt ring. Liam stood up and shook himself all over. More oil flew off but again didn't go any farther than the salt ring which was turning gray.

Liam blinked at them and then cocked his head to one side.

"Well, that ought to do it," said Diana, clearing a path through the salt and gesturing to Liam.

"He's still wolf-shaped."

"As I said, it'll take a little bit for his body chemistry to settle. A little nap and he'll back in business. You look like you could do with some sleep yourself. Why don't you two go up to bed and grab some shut-eye?"

"That sounds good," said Scarlet around a yawn. "Come on, Wolf. Bedtime."

Paxton

Paxton parked his truck and jogged easily through the woods in human form. It had taken him the better part of the morning and into the afternoon to drive to Abingdon. After that, he'd had to give in and ask in town about Mrs. Lucas. He'd had to say he was a friend of Scarlet's to make any headway with the locals. It was only after he'd said Scarlet was doing well in the city and dating his brother, and that he was delivering a present for her, that they volunteered directions out to Lucas farm.

He'd intended to simply drive up and ask for Scarlet politely, but as he'd gotten closer, he'd become less certain of that plan. So he'd parked out of sight of the white farmhouse and moved down-wind. He made his way through the underbrush and found a hint of Liam coming toward him along with Scarlet and a strong smell of lavender, sage, and another person he didn't know. There were also chickens, a goat, and a coyote out in the field somewhere.

As he watched, a woman dressed in jeans and rubber boots came out of the house and went to the barn. Guessing that this was his moment to find Liam without interference, he dashed forward and slid in the back door.

EPISODE 22

THE RIGHT THING

Liam

Liam woke up warm and wrapped around Scarlet, which was always nice. He yawned and stretched and cracked an eyelid. Then he sat up with a frown. He had no idea where he was. It was a nice-looking room, with dainty white furniture, and cheerful blue curtains that were currently pulled tight against the encroaching sunlight. He rubbed his head and tried to pull up the last thing he remembered. His canines lengthened as he remembered the warlocks on the freeway. He took a deep breath and settled himself, inhaling for any scent of danger, but there wasn't any—just too much lavender, evergreen, and sage. He smelled himself and winced. It smelled like he'd been rolling in essential oils. He had no idea what had happened, but he must be safe because Scarlet was here. He looked around the room again and then down at Scarlet. This time he almost laughed.

She sleepily opened her eyes and the smile that lit up her face hit him like an arrow from Cupid's bow. He wanted to see that smile every morning of his life.

"Where's the hat?" he whispered.

"What?"

"You need the frilly hat and you'll look like the grandmother from Little Red Riding Hood."

She giggled but didn't respond. Instead, she pulled him down and kissed him. He was fine with that. Her kiss became softer and more passionate and he was fine with that too. He reached down to find the edge of her nightgown, which was too much fabric for any sensible kind of person and worked it up, finally finding the soft skin of her thighs. He felt as if he hadn't seen her in days. He really ought to ask her what had happened, but that would mean that he would have to stop kissing her. He nuzzled into her neck, loving the way she made little pleasure noises as he nibbled at her ear. His hand was all the way up under her nightgown and he'd found the sweet spot between her legs. She was wet and made a little moan as he caressed her.

Finally, he broke away and sat up. "Off," he said, tugging at her nightgown. She made an agreeing noise and sat up, the covers falling away from her. He pulled the nightgown roughly over her head and tossed it on the floor. He was about to go back to kissing her when he caught a familiar whiff of something.

"Paxton?" he said, turning to the door in confusion.

"Liam?" barked his brother loudly, bursting through the door. Scarlet shrieked and dove beneath the covers.

"Shit!" yelled Paxton and jumped back through the door, slamming it after him. "Sorry!" Paxton yelled through the door. "Uh… Sorry. I'll be downstairs. Shit. Sorry, Scarlet!"

Liam heard the clatter of his brother's footsteps going down some stairs. Scarlet's eyes and nose appeared above the covers.

"Scarlet," said Liam. "Where are we? Why is my brother here? And most of all, where are my clothes?"

"We're at my grandma's house," whispered Scarlet, her cheeks flushed pink. "I don't know why Paxton's here. And you weren't wearing any."

"OK, that's… all very non-informative. What the hell happened?"

"We were attacked by warlocks and you got stuck in your wolf shape. And then you came to find me, but I couldn't fix you because of the protest at the trees. So, I tried to bring you to Grandma's, but we got attacked again. I think your brother came to rescue us, but I'm not entirely sure because I got knocked out. When I woke up, your mom wanted me to leave. And I think she hates me now because I threw a chair through her window. But either way, she wasn't going to let me leave with you. So, then I wolf-napped you and brought you home to Grandma and she fixed you. I don't know how Paxton got here."

Liam scratched vigorously behind his ear. Several things were clear. Scarlet knew what he was. Scarlet was not bothered by that information. Both he and Scarlet had been attacked by warlocks and Scarlet's grandmother had the skills to fix that kind of magic. Clearly, they had reached a point in their relationship where *things* were going to need to be discussed. However, the thing that seemed most abundantly clear to him was that he was about three meals short of where he needed to be.

"I think I'm too hungry for any of this," he said. "I need pants."

"Mmm… food," said Scarlet, in a tone that he'd thought reserved just for him. "I forgot about food. I want food." She sat up and looked at his raised eyebrows. "Don't give me that look. I've been busy worrying about your shit and haven't eaten since possibly yesterday. I'm starving."

"How long was I out of it?" he demanded as she climbed out of bed.

"I don't know. You came to find me on Saturday morning and I'm pretty sure it's Monday, so probably a couple of days. I tried to feed you beef jerky from the bodega on Saturday, but you didn't like it."

"Of course I didn't like it," he said making a retching face and Scarlet giggled as she rummaged through the chest of drawers.

"It was all they had that I thought you would eat." She found a sweatshirt and some sort of flannel pants and pulled them on. "OK, wait here. I'll go see if Ochre's got anything for you to wear in his room."

She came back a few minutes later with matching pajama pants to hers and a sports t-shirt from a team he didn't recognize. The pants were far too long for him.

"How tall is your brother?" he asked rolling up the pants.

"Six-five," said Scarlet. "Those are from when we did the matching Solstice pajama picture. Sorry, they're all I could find."

"Better than nothing."

He followed Scarlet down the stairs noting the family pictures along the way. It was only in the oldest picture that Scarlet's mother made an appearance. She was an ethereal-looking woman, pale and slim with arresting blue eyes. Of all the children, Scarlet resembled her the most, but he thought Scarlet was prettier, more vibrant, and full of life.

The smell of something wonderful was wafting up the stairs and Liam's mouth watered as they entered the kitchen. Paxton was sitting by a wood stove with his head hung low and Scarlet's grandmother glaring at him from the oven. She was a strong-faced woman with hair that might have been white or blonde in a long braid down her back, dressed in jeans and a puffer vest.

"Lunch will be on in a minute," she said. Then she turned around to look at them. "Oh, shoot. You put your human back on."

Liam paused mid-step, uncertain of how to respond. He had zero experience with discussing his dual body condition with anyone non-wolf.

"I was hoping you could run out and pee on some things for me," she continued.

"Grandma!"

"What? That damn coyote out there thinks my chickens are his personal buffet. I thought if he caught a whiff of something Liam's size he'd think twice."

Liam glanced at Paxton who looked frozen in shock.

"Um," said Liam. "I could probably do that."

"Could you? Be a lamb, and just hit all the fence posts. I think that ought to do it. You can change in the laundry room." She gestured to a door off to the left. "I'll have some chili when you get back."

"You don't have to," said Scarlet.

"Um," said Liam. "I have to visit the little boy's tree anyway."

Scarlet giggled.

"Yeah, OK," said Liam, feeling that he'd entered the twilight zone. "I'll be right back."

It was a nice little farm. Tidy and well organized. He ran across the crunchy snow and made his appointed pit stops before racing back up to the house. He avoided the chicken house on the way. The coyote was not wrong—the chickens did smell like lunch.

He changed back to manage the back-door handle and then slammed it quickly closed against the cold and hurried back into clothes.

"Liam," called Scarlet's grandma as he entered, "did you want biscuit or cornbread?"

"Cornbread, please," he called back. He entered the kitchen and saw that Paxton was setting the table, while Scarlet fetched glasses and her grandmother dished chili into bowls. He thought it was a venison chili from the smell and his mouth began to water once more.

"I'm sorry, ma'am," he said as she looked up. "If we were introduced last night, I don't remember."

She smiled and he caught a flash of Scarlet in her face. "I'm Diana Lucas. You can call me Diana."

"Liam Grayson," he said. "And you've met my brother Paxton."

"Ah, yes, Mr. Doesn't-Know-How-to-Knock."

"Sorry," Paxton said blushing bright red. "I only wanted…"

He trailed off looking at Liam desperately and Diana chuckled.

"Not to worry. But next time you visit, come to the front door. You'll save everyone a bit of embarrassment I think."

"Mm-hmm," said Scarlet, plunking the glasses down with extra emphasis.

"Yes, ma'am," said Paxton and grimaced apologetically at Scarlet.

The meal was one of the most pleasant Liam had ever experienced. Diana and Scarlet caught up on local gossip, with Scarlet gasping in shock at the news that Dan Weyers had installed not one, but two windmills and was now preaching the gospel of wind power at his neighbors. And then doubling down with a *bless her heart* at the news that Mrs. Winderling had left her husband after twenty years of marriage when someone finally spilled the beans about the girlfriend he'd kept on the side. Paxton's eyebrows flew up when Diana also casually mentioned that Azure's coven had been thinking about funding one of their members in her run for the state senate.

"Well, I think they should," said Scarlet. "I said it ten years ago when she tried to drag me to those stupid meetings—they either needed to do more magic or get more involved."

"The meetings are not stupid," said Diana calmly.

"Yes, well, there was a shocking lack of eye of newt. I'm just saying that if you're going to have a coven, I expect less tea and more general cursing of people. I've had more conniving and backstabbing from a gathering of cheerleaders."

"I'm sure that goes without saying," said Diana. "But the focus of the coven is environmental change, not cursing people. And having one of their members in a very public position is a risk."

"They should join Albert's super pack," said Paxton and Liam kicked him under the table.

"What?" demanded Paxton looking offended. "If there are actual witches somewhere, they sound right up Albert's alley. If you're going to go political, why stop at wolves? You and Albert want to think big, well, here's your big."

"Someone's forming a Supernatural super PAC?" demanded Scarlet. "Yes! I want in!"

"Maybe," said Liam. "It's early days. He's still building support." He looked at Scarlet's excited grin. "I'll talk to him," he promised and Scarlet clapped her hands in excitement.

"And we'll talk to Azure," said Diana, dampeningly. "As I said, I'm not sure the witches are ready for the level of publicity that politics brings. But it would be good to talk."

Liam nodded. At the moment all he could think was that witches, real witches, not the crap-jewelry, neo-pagan, peyote-pushing wannabes that seemed to be everywhere, would be a real benefit to his pack. As long as he could get his mother to see that. As if on cue, Paxton's cell phone rang with the Darth Vader theme song.

"Well, that's Mom," said Paxton. "Excuse me. I'll step out on the porch."

Scarlet glanced nervously at Liam, and he tried to smile reassuringly. Not that he had much reassurance to offer. He thought that this entire situation was going to drive his mother to declare a lock-down and bring everyone back to the house. He was probably going to have to spend a week talking her out of making him quit his job and move home.

Paxton came in a few minutes later, looking grim. "Mom says come home."

"Yeah," agreed Liam, shoveling the last of his chili in his mouth. He hadn't expected anything else.

Scarlet

Scarlet sat on the low rock wall outside the Grayson homestead, watching the sunset, and tried not to feel like forgotten luggage. She had known from Paxton and Liam's expressions that her arriving home with them was not going to go well, but she hadn't been prepared for the fact that the pack wouldn't even let her in the house. She didn't know a lot about wolf culture. She understood it as very pack-oriented with everyone living together or in near proximity to each other. She supposed that made Liam an iconoclast. She liked that he was a rebel, but at the moment she didn't like that he was having to be a rebel over her.

The lunch with Paxton and Liam had gone so well. She thought that Grandma had liked them. And Paxton had loosened up and been goofy and funny which brought out Liam's affectionate side, and that was adorable. She thought that Paxton had rolled his eyes rather hard at the way she and Liam had held hands on the ride back, but she had gotten the impression that he genuinely liked her and had been happy for Liam. Apparently, his feelings didn't transfer to their mother or the rest of the pack.

She kicked her feet against the gray rock and tried not to shiver. At least the yelling had stopped in the house. But maybe that wasn't a good sign.

Paxton

Paxton looked at his brother's face and knew that things were about to go very, very wrong. Liam had stopped looking angry several minutes ago. Now he just looked tired. Tired in a way that aged him and made him look like Dad. He knew their mother saw it too, but where Aisling thought it meant that she was winning, Paxton thought that it meant they were all about to lose.

"She cannot be here," said Aisling, and they all felt the iron Command of the Alpha resonate in her voice. Aisling rarely used that alpha gift that forced a pack member to comply, but it seemed that today she was not in a mood to be generous. Paxton had been praying that she wouldn't because he knew what that would mean to Liam. To Liam, consent was everything. If someone had to be forced into compliance then an alpha wasn't leading, they were ruling. Paxton had a saying jotted down in his notebook of Dad-isms about that and he wasted precious seconds trying to remember what the exact saying was. But his mind wouldn't supply it and it felt like busy work for his brain because he couldn't face the fact that his family was crumbling in front of him.

Paxton could see Scarlet through the window of the great room where the entire pack was gathered. The pack had been mostly silent, leaving the arguing to Aisling and Liam. Outside, Scarlet flipped one of her braids over her shoulder where it hung like a golden rope and Paxton could see the Little Red Riding Hood that Liam had fallen in love with.

"You will do the right thing," continued Aisling, her voice crackled at the edges and the entire pack winced at the way it sawed across the nerves. "You will send her home."

Liam's shoulders sagged and Paxton tensed. Liam was never going to take this. Would he challenge their mother? Paxton felt like he wanted to throw up. How was he supposed to choose?

"Mom," said Liam, wearily, looking defeated.

"You will do the right thing," she snarled.

Liam looked at Paxton and Paxton could see that the decision had been made and there was nothing he could do to change it.

"I will do the right thing," Liam repeated. "I will take her home."

Perhaps Aisling didn't notice that slight shift in Liam's words, but Paxton felt the vibration in the air. Liam was obeying the Command, but he'd done something. Something that he shouldn't have been able to do.

Liam walked out of the room and Paxton caught the faint jingle of his keyring as Liam picked up the keys to Paxton's truck. Paxton closed his eyes, wishing he didn't know what the sound meant. Liam was keeping the Command and breaking it all at the same time.

"There," said Aisling, her voice returning to normal, as the front door shut. "That will solve that."

Aunt Bryn sighed audibly and gave Aisling the kind of side-eye that was only allowed because of her age. The rest of the pack members were staring at their feet or anywhere but at their leader.

"You do understand that he's not coming back, right?" asked Aunt Bryn, at last.

"What?" Aisling looked at Bryn in confusion. "No. He will follow the Command. He said he'd do the right thing."

"He *is* doing the right thing," said Paxton. "She's his mate. You don't leave your mate."

"That's ridiculous, Paxton," said Aisling. "She's human. Wolves can't mate with humans anymore."

"She fought warlocks for him," said Devin.

"She cured him," said Uncle Marcus.

"She was going to quit her job and move to the woods for him," said Aunt Bryn.

"She got in the cage with him," said Paxton.

"She's his mate," said Conner, with a sigh that was echoed around the room. "That's how he can break the Command. He's not coming back."

"No," said Aisling, firmly, overriding their comments.

"So much for our safeguard against warlocks," muttered Derek, as he left the room.

"No," said Aisling. This time she sounded uncertain, but the pack was already leaving the room. "No, I used the Command. He will obey."

Paxton looked at his mother and wondered what his father would say, or what Liam would say. Finally, it occurred to him to wonder what he should say. He wanted to explain to his mother all the ways in which she'd fucked up. The ways that she had been a shitty parent. The ways that she had hurt him and the countless ways that she'd hurt Liam and taken him for granted. He wanted to point out how her fear of change had caused more change. How her desperate clinging to the past made the present even more untenable. How trying to force Liam to stay was the very thing that made him leave.

"He will come back," said Aisling, but it was to an empty room. "He'll come back," she said, this time to Paxton. Outside, Liam was holding out his hand to Scarlet and she was smiling up at him. She took his hand and they walked down the drive together.

"No, Mom," said Paxton. "He's not coming back and it's because of you." Paxton couldn't find the words for anything he wanted to explain and finally said the one thing that was any comfort to him. "I'm glad Dad's not here to see this."

His mother went pale, but Paxton couldn't find any sympathy for her. He turned and left the room.

EPISODE 23

BECAUSE OF YOU

Scarlet

Liam was sad. Scarlet could feel it leaking out of him in little waves. She closed her eyes and looked for the tangled red string that bound the two of them together. It was there, wrapping around each of her fingers and up her arm. He loved her as much as ever, if not more, but he was still sad.

"What do you think about moving in together?" he asked suddenly, turning away from the floor-to-ceiling window in his narrow living room. She was sitting on his couch and pretending to be watching the light fluffs of snow that were drifting out of the sky and onto the treetops in the park. Scarlet blinked at him. It sounded like a much better idea than trying to maintain her plants while commuting back and forth from Brooklyn. They were getting droopy without her. And he was next to a park so that worked out.

"We might need to find a bigger place," he said looking around.

"No, I need the green space," said Scarlet. "I mean, yes, I'll move in with you. I like your place. We can live here. I like it because it's close to the park."

"Me too," he said, smiling at her, but the sadness in his eyes didn't go away.

The drive from his family's property to the city had been mostly silent. Scarlet had gathered that whatever had happened hadn't gone well, but she was beginning to think it had gone very, very badly. They'd made the team decision to both call in sick for the day.

She had hoped he would be better by today. But his mood hadn't changed and the snow outside only seemed to bring it out further.

"Did you want to go to your Grandma's over the holidays?" he asked.

"Yes," said Scarlet. "My brother and sister will come home then. We're not Christian of course, but we do like the lights. And the food."

"And the gifts?" he asked, teasingly.

"If you're doing the food, then you might as well do the gifts," she said. "You could come too if you wanted."

"That sounds nice," he said. "I always wanted to do the Norman Rockwell Christmas."

"Oh, well, no. You're not going to get that. Azure will probably want to sing some sort of horrible holiday song about sacrificing Christians and do not even think about buying anyone anything plastic because she will make a scene. Ochre will probably get drunk and start a lecture on how the pesticides in crops are causing birth defects. And Grandma will probably want to try and go see Mom and we'll try and talk her out of it."

"Where is your mom?" asked Liam and Scarlet instantly regretted mentioning her mother.

"Uh… with my Dad. Grandma doesn't approve. You know, because she left all of us here. So… that gets super awkward."

She had explained about *traveling* to Liam and she thought he got that she wasn't entirely human and he'd seemed fine with it, but she also got the feeling that he didn't know where the boundaries were. But discussing where the Fae had gone to was one of the things that she was not allowed to talk about.

"Oh," said Liam, clearly sensing her tone. "Sorry."

"It's OK," said Scarlet. "We've talked about it. Mom's better off with him anyway. She was never any good at being here. But Grandma still gets mad."

"It's hard when our families won't behave like we want them to," said Liam. He picked at the fringe on a blanket that hung over the back of the couch and Scarlet sighed. Apparently, she wasn't good at seeing his boundaries either.

"Liam," she said, softly, "is your family not behaving like you want them to?"

"No," he said shaking his head. "*I'm* not behaving like they want me to. And so, I'm just... I'm not welcome back."

"Because of me?" asked Scarlet, tears filling her eyes.

"No. Yes. No. It's been a long time coming. I just can't do it anymore." He shook his head, tears filling his eyes too. His fingers clenched around the back of the couch and then he consciously seemed to loosen them one by one. "This isn't because of you," he said, looking directly at her. "Don't think that. It's just the situation."

Scarlet set her mug down on the coffee table and rose to her knees so she could hug him over the back of the couch. But she thought he was lying. She kept her arms locked around him and tried to figure out how to give him hope.

"All those warlocks that attacked us are dead by the way," she said. "Even the first one, that tried to attack me in the park, that cut your shoulder. He only made it three blocks. I probably ought to feel bad about that, but I don't. I feel like you're the best boyfriend ever whether you're on two or four feet."

He laughed and then leaned back to look at her face. "How many warlocks have been attacking us? I wish I could remember what the hell happened."

"Um... four? No, five. And I'm pretty sure that at least some of them were in those files you had on your desk. But that wasn't my point. My point was that I know... I know things look kind of grim now with your family, but I think if we give it a little time that maybe they'll come around."

He smiled, but she didn't think he believed her.

"And I know things have been crazy, but as long as we're together I'm pretty sure we can get through anything. warlocks, woods, or what-have-you," she said and at last his smile got bigger. "And I have missed you, my wolf," she continued, working her hands under his sweater and shirt to his skin. She stretched up to kiss him and he eased over the couch to slowly tackle her into the sofa cushions.

"How much have you missed me, Little Red?" he murmured, unbuttoning her shirt that was really a shirt of his that she'd borrowed after a shower. She'd been intending to change but hadn't gotten around to it. They weren't going anywhere, so what was the point?

"Hmmm," said Scarlet, as he ran his tongue across her collar bone. "Quite a bit?" she offered. He growled and nipped at her nipple, making her gasp and smack at his shoulder. He kissed and sucked on it penitently.

"How much did you miss me?" he asked again as he worked her underwear off, his tongue trailing across her belly.

"Very, very much, lots," said Scarlet as his tongue got closer to where she wanted it to be. He looked up at her, his eyes dancing in amusement.

"Very much lots," he said. "That's a significant amount."

"Yes," she moaned as he licked along her thigh. "So very much lots."

He laughed and then moved in closer and breathed out, warming her pussy with his breath before flicking out his tongue.

"Oh, Goddess," she moaned. His tongue was a miracle. A work of art. A thing of beauty. She rocked with his every flick and lap, giving herself up to him. She buried her hands in his hair and closed her eyes.

"Wolf, Wolf, yes, Wolf, yes!" She was half falling off the couch, panting and writhing as he brought her to peak after peak. His rhythm began to change going faster and doing whatever it was that made her tingle everywhere. She came with a gasp, clutching and clawing at Liam as they slipped off the couch and fell onto the carpet.

He rolled her over and she found herself on her hands and knees. "Wolffff, ohhhh."

He teased her with his cock, letting it drag across her pussy.

"Do you want me?" he asked and she could hear that he was smiling.

"You know I do," she gasped. "Please, Wolf, please." She was practically frantic to have him inside her, but he continued to tease her.

"Wolf," she panted, "Wolf, I swear…" she broke off as he eased into her. He groaned in pleasure and she would have agreed with him but it was all she could do to keep from dropping to the floor.

She arched as he pulled her hair and she came again. He gave her a moment and then began to pound into her in earnest. She could feel herself building again, her entire body seemed to vibrate.

"Red," he growled, "Red!"

Liam reached underneath her, put his knuckle right against her clit. With each thrust, the swollen nub hit his knuckle with pleasure generating force that left her shaking. She wanted to scream out her satisfaction but was breathless. He thrust again and again and she came with a wordless cry that left her face down in the carpeting. He came after she did and landed on top of her with a satisfied grunt.

"Scarlet," he said, quietly, wrapping his arms around her. "I love you."

"I love you too, Liam," she whispered and put a little love bite on the hand nearest to her. He growled his rumbliest, happiest growl, and Scarlet smiled.

But later, when he was asleep, she crept out of bed and snuck his phone off the dresser. Once she was in the bathroom with it, she flipped through the address book until she found Paxton's number. She wasn't sure she could fix Liam's family, but at least she could make sure he didn't lose his connection to his brother.

EPISODE 24
NEW PATHS

Paxton

Paxton stared at his room and the boxes that he'd put in it. He thought it looked believable. He began to put away all the random childhood memorabilia. He probably needed to clean out a lot of that stuff anyway. His childhood had become visual wallpaper and he needed to put it away and make room for being an adult.

"What are you doing?" demanded his mother, from the doorway.

"I am packing," said Paxton, without turning around. He moved a model airplane from the dresser and into a box.

"Putting some things away," she said, her voice refusing to make it a question.

"Some of the kid stuff, yeah," said Paxton, still refusing to turn around. "But I'm going to need all my stuff once I'm settled. Don't worry. I'll send for it as soon as I can and get it out of your hair."

"What?"

Paxton could hear the edge of anxiety in Aisling's voice, even though she was trying to mask it.

"Well," said Paxton, straightening up and staring down into a box of his childhood toys, "since you don't see fit to let Liam have his mate, and you don't think having protection against the warlocks is a good idea, I guess I just don't feel like this is the pack for me anymore." He turned around to face his mother. "I'm leaving."

"You will not," said Aisling, stepping angrily into the room. "You will not. I will make you stay."

"Are you going to use the Command on me, Mom? That didn't work too well with Liam."

"You have to stay," she said and this time he really could hear the fear in her voice. He realized now why Liam had always been so patient in his arguments with Aisling.

"Mom," said Paxton, "if Liam's not part of the pack then I don't want to be either."

"It was his choice!" she snapped. "He picked *her* over us!"

"Because you made him," said Paxton. "What would you have done if someone had made you choose between the pack and Dad?"

"She is human! It is *not* the same!"

"They say we used to be able to mate with humans," said Paxton. "Maybe Scarlet is a throwback or something. Because I'm telling you, Mom… She and Liam…"

"No!" yelled Aisling. "No! That is not what is supposed to happen! I want him to be with Anna Allanach."

Paxton sighed. "None of this is supposed to happen, Mom. It's just the way it is."

"No! I don't like it! I forbid it! I won't let it!" yelled Aisling.

Paxton felt his heartbreak a little and he stepped forward and hugged his mother. She gave an angry growl, thrashing against him, and then stopped and collapsed into him with a sob.

"Mom, I miss Dad too, but we can't stay like this. We need things to change."

"We don't need a damn human!" she snarled, stepping back, swiping angrily at her nose.

"No, but Liam does and it is your job to make sure the pack gets what it needs."

"I… No." But she didn't look as certain as she had a moment before.

"Yes," said Paxton. "Either we go get Liam back or I'm going to finish packing and move out to the city to be with him."

Aisling stared at him without moving.

"OK," said Paxton. He could feel himself sweating. He hadn't thought his mom would call him on it. He pulled open a drawer and began to pull out his t-shirts. Aisling suddenly gave a fierce snarl and stomped from the room.

"Where you going, Mom?" Paxton called after her.

"To get my damn keys. Shut up and go get in the car."

In the privacy of his room, Paxton smiled and took out his phone, and dashed off a quick text.

Plan in motion. See you soon.

Liam

It was one week before Christmas and Liam was both petrified and electrified by the idea of a holiday without his family. Being packless wasn't getting better—it was like an empty place in his soul that he hadn't known was occupied before—but Scarlet was somehow making things easier. He didn't understand how it was possible, but the longer he was with her the more certain he became that she was his mate. He'd heard other mated wolves say that it was like knowing which way was North—it was just the way it was— and that was how it felt with Scarlet. She was who he was *supposed* to be with. He scrubbed the kitchen counter and checked the clock again. Her interview was supposed to have been done by now. He'd had to stay at work for a meeting—he hadn't even been able to see her off. Knowing how badly she wanted the job made him want it for her. He wanted her to get everything she wished for and not being able to simply give it to her was torturing him. He found himself contemplating murder if the idiots at Kadry Environmental

Consultants didn't give her the position. He scrubbed the counter harder.

When he heard her key in the lock, he flung the sponge at the sink and stepped into the hall.

"Well?" he demanded.

"Nailed it," she said dropping her bags and jumping into his arms.

He kissed her, loving the way her heartbeat harder for him. He swung her around and set her on her feet again.

"Did they offer you the job on the spot?" he asked pulling her into the living room.

"No, but they showed me the office I would have and the break room and told me that I would hear from them soon. And they kind of gave the *soon* extra oomph."

"In other words," said Liam, "You nailed it."

"Yes!" she exclaimed and kissed him again.

"Let's go celebrate. Get something pretty on and we'll go to Maxim's." He grabbed her hand and gave her a little twirl.

"Will you buy me gallons of champagne and punch vampires who hit on me?" asked Scarlet, beaming up at him.

"Um… sure? If necessary? Are you planning on getting hit on by vampires?"

"No. But when I picture rowdy evenings out, that's what I picture now. I had no idea people did that before I met you."

Liam laughed. "Sure, you punch one vampire one time…"

She giggled. "What? I thought it was sexy!"

"Oh, well, then," he slid his arms around her waist. "I will punch all the vampires you want."

The doorbell rang and they both stared at the door in surprise.

"One of the neighbors probably," said Liam, going down the hall.

"Probably," agreed Scarlet. He glanced back at her as he reached for the door puzzled by the way her heart was beating faster than it should be. She was worried about a neighbor? But as his hand came to rest on the doorknob, his nose twitched and he knew that it wasn't any of the neighbors. He hesitated a long moment and then opened the door.

Paxton and their mother stood in the hallway. Liam thought he had never seen Aisling look more uncomfortable. They stared at each other. His mother looked wary. Liam's eyes flicked to Paxton, standing behind Aisling. Paxton looked smug.

"Well," said Scarlet, from behind him. He glanced over his shoulder at her. She looked determinedly cheerful. "I will go put the kettle on. Unless we all want to move straight to wine?"

"Tea is fine, Scarlet," said Paxton, stepping forward, practically pushing Aisling ahead of him. "Thanks."

Liam swung the door shut behind them and led the way into the living room. Aisling seated herself in the blue armchair and looked around the room.

"You put up one of Papa's paintings," she said, looking at the artwork over the fireplace.

Aisling's father had been an odd wolf who had enjoyed a more creative outlook on life. Liam still had his custom-crafted wolf backpack outfitted for paintbrushes and art supplies in storage somewhere.

"Yes," said Liam, realizing that she'd never been in his apartment.

"It looks nice." Aisling looked around the room—everywhere but at Scarlet who was in the kitchen getting out mugs and tea.

"Mom," said Liam, "have you met my girlfriend, Scarlet? She's moving in with me next month."

Aisling's mouth flattened out into a line.

"Nothing to say?" prodded Liam.

"The only thing I have to say on the topic is that someday you will want children and you will regret this. Other than that, I came to say that I..."

Aisling hesitated as Scarlet came into the living room carrying a tray with sugar, cream, and a selection of teas. Scarlet frowned as she set the tray down on the coffee table.

"Well, I want children," Scarlet said. "I mean, eventually. Not right now."

Liam felt struck dumb. He'd meant to cover that information at some point. But it hadn't come up.

"Wolves and humans can't mate anymore," Aisling said with a malicious smile and he'd never wanted to bite his mother more in his life.

"Oh, that's interesting," said Scarlet. "Ochre has been theorizing for years that there has been some sort of genetic transmogrification that prevents Supernaturals and humans breeding anymore. That would support his theory. But I'm not sure what that has to do with me."

"Witches are humans too," said Aisling, impatiently.

"Oh," said Scarlet. "No. I'm not... Witchcraft is a style of magic. I mean, it's got a very long tradition and rather stringent moral code, but at the end of the day, it's only a way to use power. I thought you understood..." She trailed off, looking at Liam, her eyes wide.

"Scarlet?" Liam tried to understand her reaction. Paxton abruptly burst out laughing. Everyone stared at him puzzled.

"She's not human!" exclaimed Paxton, pointing triumphantly at Scarlet.

"Don't be ridiculous," said Aisling. "She smells human. Quite nice for a human, but still human."

"Well," said Scarlet, "I'm a little human. I'm just mostly… not."

Liam scratched his head, still puzzled. "What are you then?"

"I'm Fae." Her face said she thought this was obvious. Liam couldn't say he agreed with her.

"Nonsense," said Aisling. "The Fae are all dead."

"No," said Scarlet, "they left when the humans and technology started cluttering up everything. Sometimes they come back to visit though."

"Where did they go?" asked Paxton.

"We don't really discuss that," said Scarlet.

Liam stood up because he felt like moving would be better.

"Liam?" Scarlet looked anxious. "I thought you understood because I explained about *traveling* to get to my grandmother's house."

"I knew you got there too quickly," muttered Paxton.

"I didn't know that wasn't a witch thing," said Liam, heading into the kitchen. "We don't have a lot of experience with magic. I think I'm switching to wine."

"OK," said Scarlet, but her voice wavered.

"So does this mean grandbabies or not?" demanded Aisling.

"Mom!" yelled Paxton and Liam at the same time.

"What? I want puppies!"

"Well, so do I," said Scarlet. "Just later. Once my career is firmly established."

Liam couldn't find a corkscrew so he grew a claw and jammed it into the bottle.

"I always figured I'd do the kid thing around the first time I had to retire," he said, pulling the cork out with a satisfying pop.

"Oh, that's a good idea," said Scarlet. "Take a decade or two off to concentrate on the kids and then reenter the workforce once everyone forgets we're supposed to be old? That's a good plan. Let's do that. I mean…" She looked awkwardly around at his family.

"Assuming we don't break up. I'm not saying we're having kids. I'm not assuming anything. That's just a good plan."

Aisling snorted her disbelief.

"All right, fine," said Aisling. "I withdraw my objection to this," she waved her hand dismissively, "relationship. Liam, I will expect you home for Christmas." She stood up and dusted off her hands as if to signal that the job had been completed.

"I'm going to Scarlet's for Christmas," said Liam. Behind Aisling, Paxton looked like he was trying to contain a fit of giggles.

"You're all welcome to come," said Scarlet. "You would have to sleep in the barn though. And you can't eat the chickens."

"I don't do... either of those things," said Aisling looking offended.

"Bullshit." Paxton's fake cough fooled no one and this time it was Liam who had to contain his laughter.

Aisling glared at all of them. "I am going home now. Paxton, let's go."

"Yes, Mom," said Paxton grinning. "Scarlet, it was nice to see you. Liam, I'll call you next week."

Liam waited until they were out of the apartment before turning back to Scarlet.

"I really did not get that was what you were trying to tell me."

"Well, I see that now," said Scarlet. "Are you all right with it?"

"Well no," he said downing most of his glass of wine. "Because I have been completely careless with the condoms. What if you had gotten pregnant? We're not ready for that!"

"I have a spell for that," said Scarlet. "Keeps the babies away and my hormones at really stable levels. We're good."

"Oh."

He poured another glass of wine and stared at it.

"My mother totally caved, didn't she?"

"Yes, I believe so, but she managed to do it without actually apologizing or admitting she was wrong. Which is a bit annoying," said Scarlet, frowning.

"Never going to happen," said Liam. "I'm not even sure how Paxton got her here in the first place."

"Dunno," said Scarlet with a shrug. "He probably just convinced her to listen to reason."

"Yeah…" said Liam. "Not really seeing that one happening either."

Scarlet shrugged again, but her eyebrows remained suspiciously high. She really was the worst liar.

"You called him, didn't you?"

"You were sad," wailed Scarlet. "I had to do something. And Paxton was nice to me. I figured he didn't hate me. So… I had to try. I thought maybe I could convince him to see you on the side. You know… like a side pack."

Liam couldn't stop himself from snorting in amusement.

"He said it wouldn't work though and it was just time for your mom to stop using her third shape."

"Third shape?" asked Liam, frowning.

Scarlet cleared her throat and looked guilty. "Jackass," she muttered and this time Liam couldn't stop the full-throated guffaw that burst out of him.

"Oh, God, I'm going to cry," he said wiping his eyes.

"Anyway, I don't know what he did, but I got the text that they were coming on the way home from the interview."

"Devious," said Liam, shaking his head.

"Maybe." Scarlet looked unrepentant. "But at least we're all official with your family now," she said, grinning. "And as soon as I get my new job, we can be officially official everywhere."

She came around the kitchen counter and slid her arms around his neck. Liam felt his face crack into the largest smile he'd had in days.

"I cannot believe…" He shook his head. "This is so not where I thought I would be a few months ago."

"Well, Wolf, that's what you get for talking to strange girls you meet in the forest," said Scarlet primly.

"Little Red," he said, leaning down to kiss her. "I do believe that you have completely lured me off my path."

"Have I?" she asked, her eyes going big and round and innocent. "No, it couldn't be. Everyone knows I'm the good girl."

"Very good," he agreed, kissing her again. "Very good, indeed."

EPISODE 25

AFTERWaRD

Liam

Liam skimmed through the final page of the report and hit send.

"Mr. Grayson," said his new secretary, giving a soft knock to his open door. Her name was Delores, and she smelled of menthol cough drops and wore a lot of cardigans. She was efficient, had three kids, and gave zero fucks about being friends with him or knowing about his personal life. In other words, she was perfect. "I just got a warning flare that Brett is pissed about something and heading your way."

"I'm expecting him," said Liam, with a smile. "Don't worry about it. Go ahead and let him in."

"All right," she said with a nod.

Moments later Brett stomped into the room, slamming the door behind him.

"You got something to say to me?" demanded Brett, waving the sheaf of papers that Liam had left on his desk.

"I thought those pretty much spoke for themselves," said Liam, standing up.

"What the hell is this?" growled Brett.

"It's your twenty-minute head start," said Liam.

"What?" Brett paused, eyes narrowing suspiciously.

"Those are the emails from you to Applecourt that you tried to delete off the main server. You were helping him and those emails prove it. At the end of the week, I'm going to be sending them to our legal department and Grant. I'm showing them to you now as a courtesy—to give you the opportunity to resign."

"I'm not going anywhere," snarled Brett, striding forward to lean on Liam's desk.

"Oh, Brett, you really ought to reconsider," said Liam, smiling. "After all, I'm pretty sure you'll need some family leave time to deal with your cousin's funeral. Or haven't they released his body from the morgue yet?"

Brett licked his lips and hesitated.

"Your cousin was Sam Hubbard, right? Did time for assault? Card-carrying Nazi party member and the Temple of the Unified Vision?"

"I barely talk to that side of the family," said Brett, backing off a half-step. "I don't know what they're up to."

"But you told him about me, didn't you? And you pulled Scarlet's HR file—found out where she lived? You gave him that address?"

"I saw the way the two of you looked at each other. You were banging your secretary. I figured a little blackmail wouldn't hurt."

"Blackmail? You think that's what was going on?"

A look of worried confusion flashed across Brett's face and Liam could smell the sour stink of fear on him. Brett hadn't known what his cousin was up to, maybe he'd suspected it was a little more than blackmail, but he hadn't questioned it. And that was why all he got was a head start.

"Brett," said Liam, baring his teeth in what might have been a smile, "you're going to quit or I'll do to you what I did to Sam."

Brett took a step back, breathing heavily. "They said Sam was torn apart by coyotes or wild dogs or something."

"Or something," said Liam, with a genuine smile this time.

"If I were you, I would run far and run fast. Leave the state. Maybe you'll make it."

"You are threatening me," said Brett. "These are threats. I'm going to have you arrested."

"No," said Liam. "You're going to quit your job and you're going to leave town. And if you're gone by the end of the week, then maybe I won't push those out to legal."

"You fucking bastard," said Brett.

"Yes," said Liam. "I really am. So don't cross me."

Brett hesitated a moment longer, and then he balled up the papers and threw them at Liam, but they unfurled halfway and fluttered uselessly onto Liam's desk. Brett stormed from the room, slamming the door behind him so hard the wall rattled.

Liam picked up the ball of papers and smoothed them out before feeding them to the shredder one by one. He had just finished the last paper when his cell phone rang.

"Liam Grayson," said Liam, picking up.

"Oh, no wait, I think I got this."

Liam smiled, recognizing the voice.

"Ha! OK, I am using the speaker function."

"Good job," said Liam.

"Hi, it's Albert DeSandre. From Oregon," Albert added as an after-thought.

"Hi, Albert."

"I got your email thing. That is some very exciting news about witches wanting to join my super pack!"

"Well, it's only the one, right at the moment," said Liam. "But she's interested in talking more."

"Good! I want witches. I want everyone. You're sure she's a real witch though, right?"

"Yes," said Liam. "She was responsible for the tree protest you were talking about last time you were here. And I have... other evidence. So yes. Definitely a witch. She'll have to fill you in on anything else. That's not my place."

Albert paused, reading between the lines. "Got it."

"One of her coven is running for state senate on an infrastructure platform and wants to put in wildlife bridges and corridors. So that's probably her most immediate interest."

"Fantastic! This is what I'm talking about!" Liam could practically hear the fist-pump over the phone. "Tell her to come out and talk to us."

"I'll set it up," promised Liam, crossing his fingers that this wasn't going to blow up in their faces. Scarlet was so excited about the possibilities that he didn't want to disappoint her, but he knew wolves and nothing moved fast in pack politics. And he also hadn't wanted to say it, but he got the impression that Azure hadn't wanted to go.

"I'll call some people," said Albert. "I've got some other interested parties. This is going to be the start of something big. I can feel it."

"I hope so," said Liam. "I really hope so."

At lunchtime, Liam put on his suit jacket and went out to his secretary's desk.

"I'm meeting my girlfriend for lunch," he said, straightening his tie. "But go ahead and call if anything comes up."

"Of course," said Delores, without looking up from her typing. He loved that she didn't care.

Scarlet was waiting for him in the park. She was sitting on a red and white checked tablecloth with plates set out and a picnic basket that looked straight out of a fairy tale illustration.

She was leaning back on her hands with her legs stretched out in front of her and her high-heels kicked off into the grass. It was too cold still for picnics, so they were the only ones out, but as he stepped off the path, the temperature grew noticeably warmer. By the time he reached the tablecloth, he had to take off his jacket.

"Warming spell?" he asked.

She tilted her head to look up at him, blonde hair falling behind her in a waterfall of gold.

"I figured out how to pull all the greenhouse gases in the immediate area into one location. It's a mini-global warming spell."

"Isn't that bad?" he asked, chuckling. She looked so pleased with herself.

"It would be, except it will burn itself out and then the area will be cleaner. It's like I'm eight extra trees right now. I'm going to have to email Azure about it. She'll love it."

"You are practically a forest," he said sitting down next to her and leaning over to give her a kiss. Scarlet giggled happily as she broke away from him.

"I talked to Albert today," he said. "Azure is officially invited to the Supernatural summit."

"Yay! Azure is going to be so excited."

Liam nodded and looked down at the tablecloth and then at the picnic basket. Food was set out on plates, but the basket, with the red and white check napkin over the top, still looked full. He flipped back the cover on the basket, inside was a slim economics textbook.

"Little Red," he said, "just where do you think we'll be using that?"

"Well," she said, clearing her throat and looking anywhere, but him, "I thought we could *travel* a teeny tiny bit into the woods and then pop right back."

"Not exactly right back?" he suggested. "Maybe stick around for a teeny tiny bit of naked time?"

She grinned guiltily and put one finger up to her lips. "Maybe?"

"Scarlet," he said and swept her other hand out from under her so that she tumbled backward onto the tablecloth with another giggle. "You are luring me into the woods again."

Scarlet wrapped her arms around him.

"Yes, Wolf," she said. "Yes, I am."

The End

Find out what happens next in...

A DEEPER BLUE

3 COLORS TRILOGY BOOK 2

EPISODE 1
Montana

Azure

Azure Lucas stepped out of the station somewhere in Montana to await her connecting train to Oregon. The train station was a flat tarmac of hopelessness and cars that stunk of oil. Or maybe that was just her mood. She had accepted that visiting Oregon was to be her penance for endangering her sister a few months earlier, but that didn't make her happy about it. Azure didn't really think that some werewolf's dream of a Supernatural Super PAC was going to come to anything. In her experience, trying to rope any of the Supernatural *others* into doing anything to make changes in the world was next to impossible. It wasn't that she didn't want this summit of the Supernatural to be a beautiful meeting of the minds and potentially world-changing—she just didn't think it was going to happen. At barely thirty, Azure found it a little bit sad that she was so jaded, but having the second sight *and* common sense made her the least romantic person she'd ever met.

The second sight—that ever-present sixth sense that would periodically grant her glimpses of the future, insight into the people around her, and a chance to change destiny—was like a semi-permanent itch in the back of her brain. And like any other itch, she was only somewhat in control of it. Sometimes, she could call it to heel, and it would answer her questions, and sometimes… sometimes it shoved information into her skull or, even worse, dropped out entirely, usually when she needed it most. And currently, when she asked the magic eight ball in her head about the summit, it said: *very doubtful.*

Azure sighed and rubbed the spot behind her ear that sometimes relieved the pressure. The second sight wasn't always her friend. She'd listened to it a few months ago about a protest against a logging company. She'd seen that there was an opportunity to change things, but there was just one catch: she'd needed her sister Scarlet to tip the balance from *could change the world* to *would change the world.* But Scarlet showing up meant danger for Scarlet. Azure had known that, and she'd gone ahead anyway.

And she'd won. The trees had been saved. Hearts had changed. And Scarlet had been OK. Mostly. Except that Scarlet's weakened state after the protest had left her and her wolf boyfriend vulnerable to being attacked by warlocks.

Every time she thought about Liam Grayson, Azure had to stretch her head to the left and right in an attempt to make her jaw unclench. Scarlet was over the moon about him. Azure was trying to withhold judgment, but she failed to see how everyone could be OK with Scarlet moving in with a guy she'd barely been dating a few months. Not to mention that Liam had been Scarlet's boss. How was that OK? Azure predicted that it would end in disaster, and then she was sure to be called away from something important to help Scarlet move out. The second sight didn't show that at all, but Azure's common sense definitely did.

Admittedly, Liam did appear to be trying very hard to be helpful by setting up this meeting with one of the oldest wolf packs on the continent. Wolf packs were notoriously private, but everyone had heard of Albert DeSandre and the Portland pack, and the fact that they were taking this extraordinary step should have been exciting. But the second sight was giving the meeting a hard thumbs down, and because of that, Azure was having a hard time working up enthusiasm for the trip.

Most of the other passengers headed across the street to a family restaurant that might have been an Applebee's at some point but now was independently owned. The new owners had strung a banner over the old sign location that read Family Food—as if that was a restaurant name.

She looked across the blacktop to a cluster of stores and shops that surrounded the train station—her other options were a grocery store that looked filthy and a pool hall with a string of motorcycles parked in front of it.

Magic eight-ball head wanted her to go to the pool hall, common sense thought that seemed like a bad plan, but second sight did not care. She looked back at the Family Food place and debated ignoring the second sight. She always had a choice.

With a sigh, Azure hoisted her one piece of luggage—a durable black backpack—higher on her shoulders and headed for the bar. The second sight was her gift, her calling, and her burden. She tried her best to do it justice, but sometimes she just wished she could have a night off. The massive bouncer at the door raised his eyebrows, but she stared him down and went inside.

The bar was everything she'd expected from outside. Which she found strangely soothing. She liked all the pot-bellied old men shooting pool dressed in more leather than a gay pride parade. She probably wouldn't like them if they started talking to her, but the second sight said that wouldn't be a problem. There were a fair number of younger guys in the room too, but the mood was mellow. The smell of French fries wafted out of the kitchen and pool balls clacked against each other under hanging pendants that spotlighted the tables and left everything else in the gloom. She looked around and decided that second sight was on top of things.

She parked herself up at the bar and smiled at the bartender.

"Hey," he said. "What can I get you?"

"What's good?"

"Well, we've got a local pale ale on tap and an elk taco plate that people seem to like."

"Elk tacos and beer," said Azure. "I'm in."

"Coming up," said the bartender.

The elk tacos turned out to be what she needed. Not to mention the beans and rice that she was pretty sure had been made with about eight pounds of butter. She was on her second beer and third taco when a text popped through from Scarlet.

ARE YOU STILL ON THE TRAIN? IS IT AWFUL?

JUST MADE IT TO MONTANA. WAITING ON A TRANSFER TO MY NEXT TRAIN. ELK TACOS, THOUGH.

She took a picture of the remaining taco and sent it.

Azure didn't want to admit it, but her family had been right. Azure had risked Scarlet's life at the protest. Their grandmother Diana had emphasized that point with a raised eyebrow and a look. Their brother Ochre had taken her out for a beer and said it quietly and a little bit sadly in a way that made Azure writhe with hot twists of guilt. It didn't matter that Azure had thought that she could protect her sister by building a foolproof spell that had turned out to be not so infallible because, as usual, Scarlet had refused to stay within the boundaries. And it didn't matter that the cause had been just or that Scarlet would have helped anyway. The point was that Azure had skipped the step where she asked Scarlet for help, permission, and consent. Azure had focused on the future and forgotten that there was a whole lot of present between here and there. The second sight was always accurate, but it didn't always spell out the consequences.

YUM! LET ME KNOW THE SECOND YOU GET TO OREGON! I'M SO EXCITED ABOUT THIS. CAN YOU LIVE STREAM WHILE YOU'RE THERE?

Reluctantly, Azure smiled. As always, Scarlet's enthusiasm was infectious.

PROBABLY NOT. UNLESS YOU WANT THEM TO EAT MY PHONE.

THEY MIGHT NOT KNOW WHAT A PHONE IS. SOME OF LIAM'S PACK SEEM KIND OF TECHNO-PHOBIC.

Azure took a sip of the beer and sighed. The worst part was that Scarlet wasn't even mad at her. Because Scarlet didn't hold grudges and thought the cause was as worthwhile as Azure did. Azure wanted to be like that, but she found that every time Scarlet bounced off to some grand new adventure that she gritted her teeth and waited for it to implode. Scarlet always got to leap first and look never, counting on Azure to catch her and clean up the mess. Azure sometimes wondered if she'd developed second sight to protect her little sister out of an evolutionary necessity. Only this time, it hadn't been Azure—it had been Liam protecting Scarlet. That thought burned too.

Someone pushed up to the bar, squishing in between her and the couple next to her, slamming large hands down on the bar top. She glanced over at him. He was tall and ripped—biceps stretching out his gray Henley that was pushed up to the elbows—with a dark brown beard and tattoos covering his forearms. He was carrying a black motorcycle jacket that he threw onto the bar, ignoring the annoyed glares of the couple as they moved their drinks further down the bar.

"Emilio!" he barked at the bartender.

"Yeah, Rafe, I see you!" the bartender yelled back. "Give me a sec!"

She guessed his name was Rafe, which was unusual but interesting.

Azure looked more closely at the tattoo on the arm closest to her and frowned. There was a symbol buried in a wave that looked suspiciously like a Fae rune for protection. She realized that she had been staring for longer than was polite and also that he had noticed. She looked into his eyes and found herself caught by their color, which was green with darker striations like celadon glazing on pottery.

"Nice tattoo," she said, looking for something that didn't make her sound like an idiot.

"Sweetheart," Rafe said, looking down at her. "I wish I had the time, I really do, but I don't."

"Oh, OK," said Azure, rolling her eyes and restraining herself from adding the word *asshole* to the end of her sentence.

She had just turned back to her last taco when her second sight kicked in hard. She swung her barstool around, grabbed Rafe by the shirt collar, and yanked him toward her just as a black eight ball zipped through the air where his head had been, smashing three bottles of booze and burying itself in the mirror behind the bar.

Rafe was now wedged between her thighs, his face inches from hers.

"You know, when you're right, you're right," he said. "I should make the time."

Then he kissed her.

A DEEPER BLUE
3 COLORS TRILOGY BOOK 2

A witch, a wolf, and the open road... no future is guaranteed.

Fae witch and seer Azure Lucas is on her way to a summit of shifters and magic-wielders in Portland, Oregon at her family's insistence. She doesn't think anything will come of it—the Supernaturals are notoriously independent and uncooperative, even when the fate of the world is on the line. But on a layover in Montana Azure collides with shifter Rafe DeSandre. A biker and lone wolf who thinks that destiny has passed him by, Rafe has no pack, no mate, and no future—he cares for himself and not much else. Yet, when the father he hasn't spoken to in decades asks for a favor, Rafe agrees to deliver a precious package to the same summit that Azure is attending. Before the unlikely duo can hit the road, they are attacked by the Warlocks—a vicious magic-wielding motorcycle gang. As the pair flee cross-country they soon find that they might be more alike than they thought and the witch who likes to plan everything and the wolf who likes to wing it might just be perfect for each other. But as Azure and Rafe prepare to battle the evil Warlocks, Azure realizes that while she and Rafe might be destined for each other, she can see that destiny might not include survival. Azure is on a collision course with fate, and she's fighting for her life, her love, and her future.

Dear Reader

Word-of-mouth is crucial for any author to succeed. If you enjoyed the book, please leave a review on your favorite book sales or review site. Even if it's just a sentence or two. It would make all the difference and would be very much appreciated. Search for: Bethany Maines on any book review site such as Goodreads, BookBub, Amazon and more.

Thank you!

About the Author

Bethany Maines is the award-winning author of action adventure and fantasy tales that focus on women who know when to apply lipstick and when to apply a foot to someone's hind end. When she's not traveling to exotic lands, or kicking some serious butt with her black belt in karate, she can be found chasing after her daughter, or glued to the computer working on her next novel.

Other Works by Bethany Maines

Carrie Mae Mysteries
Bulletproof Mascara (#1)
Compact With The Devil (#2)
Supporting The Girls
A Carrie Mae Mini-Mystery
Power Of Attorney
A Carrie Mae Mini-Mystery
High-Caliber Concealer (#3)
Glossed Cause (#4)

Tales from the City of Destiny
Short Story Collection

Wild Waters
A Paranormal Suspense Romance

The Deveraux Legacy
The Second Shot (#1)
The Cinderella Secret (#2)
The Hardest Hit (#3)
The Fallen Man (#4)

Galactic Dreams
When Stars Take Flight (Vol.1)
The Seventh Swan (Vol. 2)
The Beast of Arsu (Vol. 3)

San Juan Islands Murder Mysteries
An Unseen Current (#1)
Against the Undertow (#2)
An Unfamiliar Sea (#3)

Shark Santoyo Crime Series
Shark's Instinct (#1)
Shark's Bite (#2)
Shark's Hunt (#3)
Shark's Fin (#4)
Peregrine's Flight (#5)
Shark's Blood (#6)

Find out more at:
BethanyMaines.com

www.ingramcontent.com/pod-product-compliance
Lightning Source LLC
Chambersburg PA
CBHW051120260626
47170CB00005B/1594